Do not move. They can't s
The wind roared like a fr
tracks, straight for them. .... as the
massive ebony coach pulled by its two mammoth black bears
burst through the clouds. *They can't see you if you do not
move.* She prayed for divine intervention, even as she
watched death coming for her.

The bears stopped, and snuffled the air. They couldn't find
her. She was safe.

There was movement to her left. Terror gripped her throat,
as little Megan ran straight for her. The bears turned as one,
and sped straight toward the little girl.

Do not move. Do not move. Do not move. Even as the words
ran through her mind, Alicia leapt toward the child.

She snatched the startled child into her arms, and stumbled,
rolling as she fell to protect the child with her own body.
Coming to a sudden stop, she sat up with the whimpering
child tucked safely against her chest.

Thunder roared in her ears, as the bears' hot breath brushed
her cheek. Megan whimpered. Alicia knew if they stayed
were they were Megan would die. She couldn't live with the
death of another innocent on her conscience.

There was a flicker of movement in her peripheral vision.
He stood there; Tall, Egyptian, and wearing only a loincloth
that did nothing to hide his manhood. His tanned body
rippled with muscles, and flames flickered in the golden sun
tattooed on his broad chest. His eyes locked with hers, and
she stopped breathing. Heat pooled at her center, and her
blood ran hot. Alicia melted beneath the radiating heat of
those golden orbs. He silently offered his hand.

Alicia's eyes flickered to the fluttering nostrils of the giant
bear, and back to the nearly naked god.

Lynn Marie Simpson

Blood
Connection

Pine Lake Books
West Guilford

ISBN: 978-0-9813539-2-0
Pine Lake Books

West Guilford
www.pinelakebooks.webs.com
pinelakebooks@gmail.com

DEDICATION

To the keeper of my heart

ACKNOWLEDGEMENTS

As always I want to thank my family for being there with me on this journey.
I would like to thank Penny for her cover illustration. As always you did a great job.

Thanks

Other books by Lynn Marie Simpson

Blood Curse, 2008 by Publish America
ISBN: 1-60672-220-4

Prelude

She awoke with a jerk. Fear thrummed through her veins, as her eyes furtively searched the room for the reason she was awake.

Nothing.

She relaxed slightly, and listened to the sound of a train barreling down the tracks. *Wait a minute.* Was that a tornado? Yesterday she watched a news program where a tornado swept through a small town leaving behind a trail of destruction. Everyone the reporters talked to said it sounded like a train screaming through the sky over their heads. Besides, there were no trains anywhere near the ranch. There wasn't a whole lot of anything near the ranch.

The ranch lay in a densely wooded area in the foothills of the Catskill Mountains, about five miles from the nearest public road. South of the ranch lay the Ashokan Reservoir, and west of them was the town of Phoenicia. There was a train station in Phoenicia, but the tracks didn't come anywhere near the ranch. Not many strangers came visiting, partially due to the fact that the exact position of the ranch was a well guarded secret and accessible only by all terrain vehicles, horseback, or air. She supposed that one could hike out to the ranch, but for some reason the hikers avoided this area. She remembered the first time she came to the ranch with Aunt Althea. The closer they drew to her new home, the more intense the desire to turn and run; to go anywhere as long as it was far away from where they were going. Then Althea had wrapped her warm, soft fingers around Alicia's smaller ones, and squeezed.

"You belong here child," she whispered, and the oppressive feeling vanished, allowing Alicia to see the beauty of what was to be her home for the time being.

There were several Jeeps, a Hummer, and a couple of smaller ATV's in the large barn, but they seldom used the vehicles. Alicia's favorite mode of transportation was by horse because riding on a horse reminded her of her other life. Before her parents were murdered, and before Jade adopted her, Alicia lived on a small farm in Mexico where their only modes of transportation were by foot, and by mule.

Alicia lifted a corner of the Disney princess curtains, and peeked out the window beside her bed, careful not to wake her German-shepherd pup that slept peacefully on the foot of her bed. What she saw made her gasp, and she started to whimper.

Do Not Move. It was a command, one that she followed instinctively. *If you don't move they won't see you.* The harsh voice soothed and quieted her, even as she watched the two giant black bears, their heads turning first to the right, and then to the left. She could hear them snuffling as they tasted the air, searching for her scent. She knew that the voice was right, and that if she moved they would discover her. She stopped breathing. She became a statute, not moving, even her heartbeat slowed as she watched in mixed fear, and wonder.

The two black bears pawed the air before them like two great steeds dancing anxiously, blowing smoke out their nostrils with each exhale. The bears pulled a giant, black coach, its only color the grotesque gold inlay around the doors and windows depicting thousands of souls screaming in agony.

Where are you girl? Show yourself to me. The spirit voice crawled through her mind, like ants crawling through a picnic, even as it thundered around her making the house shake. She wanted to look, to see if anyone else heard it, but fear held her immobilized.

She would not betray her presence this time. This time she would stay quiet, and protect her new family.

Suddenly both bears turned as one, and stared straight at her. They could see her through the wall. She knew they could. She could feel their eyes burning into her soul.

I see you. The voice dripped with smug satisfaction.

Alicia screamed.

One

I *see you.*
 Alicia sat up with a jerk, and pulled the covers to her neck. Her breath came in short, quick gasps, and her body felt chilled even in the eighty-degree heat.

It was here.

She could not stop the trembling in her limbs. She had to go. For a heartbeat, white-hot anger coursed through her veins. *Why me?* The questions raced through her mind in a matter of seconds. *What did I do to deserve this nightmare? Why can't you just go away and leave me alone?*

Just as quickly as the anger flared, it vanished. She knew what it wanted—what they all wanted.

Her death.

Well it would not be long now, and they would have their wish. Only it would not be on their terms. She had always been small for her age, and pale, but at least she had been healthy. Then three months ago she started getting horrendous headaches accompanied by flashes of light, and hallucinations. At first she had been afraid that she was going blind, but after numerous tests the only thing the doctors could agree on was *she was dying*. It wasn't cancer, at least not any cancer they had come across before. With all their modern equipment they couldn't detect any tumor. Still her headaches persisted, and she grew weaker with each passing day. She was hungry all the time, but food upset her stomach. There was a very good chance she wasn't going to see her twenty fifth birthday, and her biggest regret was that she wouldn't see her family again. Never tease her brothers, or sneak out of the house with her sister. Although she was nearly a decade older, the two girls were closer than most sets of twins.

What did it matter now? She had been nothing but trouble since she was born.

Alicia? The familiar and beloved spirit voice of her little sister broke through her reverie. *Are you all right? I feel pain. Has someone hurt you?* She should have realized that Emerald would sense her pain, even at such a distance. Emmy was such a strong empath that she had trouble tuning out the emotions of strangers. When it came to her family she had only to think of them, and she could pick up what they were feeling, and thinking, although she tried very hard to tune out the latter. Not an easy task as Alicia remembered from her own youth.

I'm fine, Emmy. Alicia forced a calm she did not feel into her own spirit voice. She spoke freely with her sister, on a path shared only by her family. A path developed over many years.

At seventeen, Emerald still looked up to, and adored her older sister, and it wasn't just because Alicia always sided with her against her domineering brothers. Two against the world was their motto. Long after Emerald was more than capable of looking after herself, she still looked to Alicia for aid when it came to her brothers. Sometimes it was hard to believe that they were triplets. Quinn and Gheorgès were both tall, dark, and even though they were going through their awkward age, already extremely handsome. Emerald was slightly taller than Alicia which wasn't hard considering Alicia's own small stature, she was slender, moved with the grace of a swan, and had white blonde hair with streaks of gold and silver; the mark of the *Moarte*. She was already very powerful, and by the time she came of age she would be one of the most powerful creatures on earth.

You're not coming. Emerald said petulantly. She did not wait for Alicia to answer. *That is so not fair. I have been looking forward to this for months. Quinn and Gheorgès are so beastly to me when you aren't here. They treat me like a child.*

Alicia was supposed to meet with her family in Willow Bend to celebrate her birthday. A quarter of a century was a big deal, and her family did not know that she would probably never see it. She had said nothing about the headaches, or the doctor appointments, not wanting them to drop their lives and run to her. God she missed them. For a fleeting moment she actually considered going. What better way to spend her final days than with family and friends. The Inner Sanctum and Charlotte were in Willow Bend.

Charlotte was the woman who ran the Inner Sanctum. The Inner Sanctum was a six thousand square foot replica of a fourteenth century Romanian castle, built on a two-acre treed lot between a lake and the mountains. The stone structure could pass for Dracula's castle, and was a place of sanctuary for mortals, and most importantly immortals. Charlotte liked to tell the story of how the first settlers from Romania had built the castle stone by stone—although she never made mention of the fact that the first settlers were Lycans. Funny thing was that if you asked any of the original settlers, they would tell you that the castle just appeared there one morning, and has been there ever since.

Alicia spent a lot of time at *The Inner Sanctum* when she was a child. Her adoptive father Luke Wulfson was once the Alpha of the Willow Bend Pack of Lycans, and the family still returned there for yearly retreats. Luke had given his mansion to the Pack for the use of the single pack members, and so they stayed at the *Sanctum*. It was a comfort zone.

A safe zone.

You will not be safe there, her inner voice whispered, and she knew the truth. Nobody could stop the inevitable, not even her mother. And if the evil that stalked her while she slept and was vulnerable found her it would find her family. No, she could not go to Willow Bend, and risk their safety.

She had to disappear.

Alicia was not immune to heartbreak, but it was better the heartbreak of not seeing her family, than the heartbreak of seeing her family slaughtered—again. The memory of helplessly watching while another monster had drained the life from her precious Papa still haunted her. She had survived her first encounter with evil thanks to the *Moarte* who had rescued, and then adopted her, but neither of her parents had survived, and no matter how many times they told her it was not her fault, she knew they were wrong. It was her fault. She was the one who had reached out to a stranger. She was the one who had led that monster straight to her family.

Well this time it would be different. This time when the monster found her, for there was no doubt in her mind that it would, she would be alone. There was no way Alicia Martinez Wulfson would be responsible for the death of another person, especially when it was inevitable that she die anyway.

I am sorry, Emmy, but something has come up. Besides, you are smarter than your brothers. You only need to out think them. If she didn't leave soon she was going to change her mind and fly straight to Willow Bend, and the ones she loved. *I have to go, Em. I have a plane to catch.*

Alicia snapped her mind shut, slipped from her bed, showered, and dressed. Fifteen minutes later she was packed and on her way. She did not stop to say goodbye to anyone. She already said her goodbyes last night at her going away party. As far as everyone here knew, she was going home for a short vacation before heading for a dig in Egypt. That had been the plan before her diagnosis. Nobody knew that she had turned down the coveted position so she could spend the last few weeks of her life with her family.

You are not alone. Alicia smiled at the gruff voice, the only voice she had never been able to block from her thoughts. This was her guardian angel, her life line to sanity.

No, she was not alone, even though she dared not answer.

At the airport, she purchased a ticket for Romania. There was a dig at the foot of the Fagarus Mountains she wanted to check out. Even if there weren't a dig, she would have chosen to go there. It was the birthplace of her adoptive father, Lykos Wulfson. If she could not be with him, she could at least feel closer by touching the soil he had touched.

Alicia wiped the sweat from her brow, and looked out the window as the plane took off. She marveled at the scenery below, and was thankful to have seen the wonders she had seen. At twenty-four, Alicia was already a respected archeologist. She had been on numerous digs since the age of sixteen. For as long as she could remember, she had been fascinated with other countries, and cultures. When others her age were reading teen mysteries and romances, she was reading mysteries of another kind.

Mysteries of the dead.

She had an affinity for it. The dead spoke to her. They didn't exactly come up to her and say, " Good day, Alicia. How are you today?" It was more like watching a video playing in her head, in fast forward. When she stood on or near a grave she saw the life, and death, of the person buried there. They called to her, often leading her to the exact spot she needed to be. It was this uncanny ability of hers to find those long dead and buried that helped to build her reputation, opening doors which otherwise might be left closed to her.

If any of her colleagues felt she was too young for the job, they changed their opinion after working with her. With her sixth sense, and her meticulously thorough attitude, she soon won them over.

She had been lucky enough to have seen and done more than an average person would in an entire lifetime. Her only regret was not seeing her family again.

You will see them again, little one. This I promise you. He was wrong. She would not see them again in this lifetime, but at least they were alive.

With her forehead pressed against the cool glass, Alicia let her eyelids drop, shutting out the vanishing earth. She felt more alone on this plane full of strangers, than she had as a child living with her parents in the wilds of Mexico. Thinking about her childhood opened the floodgates of memory.

"Stop, Papa," she screamed at him with her mind. Her body and voice held immobile by the monster with the face of an angel that beckoned her father to it with a crooked finger. Her father's movements were jerky and awkward, like a puppet's, as he inched closer to the monster. His eyes glazed over and he was unaware of anything around him.

Alicia wanted to turn away from that hideously handsome face, the face of a demon, as her beloved papa stood in front of the beast, and docilely tilted his head to one side baring the rapidly beating pulse at his neck. The beast's smile widened, and its fangs grew until they were too large for its mouth, distorting its features grotesquely.

Those fangs glistened obscenely in the night, dripping a vile liquid that seared all that it touched. The monster leaned forward, and sank those horrid fangs into the vein offered so meekly by Papa. Alicia continued to stare unable to turn away or even close her eyes, as the beast drank Papa's life from his veins. The monster withdrew its fang's from Papa's neck, and as Papa's lifeless body fell noiselessly to the ground it held Alicia's gaze, and slowly licked the crimson drops from its fangs.

Alicia's head jerked and she blinked rapidly several times to clear the image from her mind. *I'm so sorry, Papa*, she whispered against the cold pane of glass. She was responsible for his death, and the death of her beloved Mama. She was the one the monster had come for. Her entire life she had heard the thoughts of those around her. Sometimes their thoughts were clearer than their actual voices, making it difficult to know when a person had spoken aloud, or merely had a passing thought.

Her abilities had terrified her parents, who took her to the more remote parts of Mexico where it was less likely anyone would find out about her. Alicia had tried to be a good girl, and not listen to the voices in her head, but she did not know how to shut them out. At first, she thought she was just like everyone else, until she discovered that nobody around her knew what she was thinking.

Until the fateful day when her entire world turned upside down; the day her thoughts led a monster straight to their door. He had been toying with her when he destroyed her parents, and he made sure she knew it. They were simply appetizers, while she was the main course. If the *Moarte* had not come when she did, Alicia would have died on her eighth birthday. Instead, the *Moarte* destroyed the vampire, rescued Alicia, and gave her a new home and family.

God she missed them already, but there was no way she was going to risk their lives because she did not want to be alone. She owed them that, and so much more.

Alicia was fascinated with ancient history. When she was nine she began reading everything she could get her hands on to do with ancient civilizations, and their languages. She had an exceptionally high IQ, and discovered that she had a photographic memory. To help feed her thirst for knowledge, Jade arranged for her to have private tutors. By the time she was eleven, she had read nearly every book on the subject, and was completely captivated with the idea of being an archeologist.

When Alicia was twelve, Jade took her to attend a seminar on archeology at the University of Leicester, in England. That was the day she knew for certain that she would be an archeologist. At home, Alicia immersed herself even more in her schoolwork, and research. She graduated high school with honors at the age of fourteen, and enrolled at the University of Leicester at the age of fifteen, signing up for as many ancient history and archeology courses possible. Languages came easily to her, and by the time she was sixteen she was fluent in English, French, German,

Romanian, and Latin. By eighteen, her fluency included Polish, Egyptian, and Ancient Greek. She was expert in hieroglyphics, which was the reason they chose her over some of her more established colleagues for the Egyptian dig. What she wouldn't give to find out what the ancient Egyptians had to tell her, literally.

When Alicia was sixteen, she was the youngest intern on a summer dig in Belize. That was when the dead first spoke to her. It was also when her nightmare stalker returned. She did not need her guardian angel to tell her to be still. Fear held her in its icy grip, and she could barely breathe. She did not dare tell anyone about the nightmares. Jade would have insisted she come home. That was something she was not about to do. Nothing short of a death in the family could have dragged her from her dream.

She did leave Leicester. With the help of several tutors, and the internet, Alicia graduated with her BA in Ancient History and Archeology, while managing to attend several digs around the world. Whenever the *Seeker*, as she grew to think of her stalker, got too close she simply moved on. Perhaps, deep down, Alicia thought she would discover something to help her fight the evil thing that stalked her. Her inner voice insisted she go to Egypt. The answers were there amongst the pyramids.

What did it matter now? She was dying. She could not change that simple fact. All she could do now was stay one step ahead of the *Seeker*, and keep that evil from her loved ones. The *Seeker* had been hunting her for years, seeking the miniscule powers she possessed—the ability to hear thoughts, move small objects with her mind, and communicate with the dead. She could not imagine what it would do if it got scent of the *Moarte*.

You do not have to die. Come to me, her angel said.

Tears filled Alicia's dark eyes, and escaped down her cheeks. She did not bother to brush them away. She could not go to him. She did not dare.

Two

Alicia quickly found a taxi willing to take her to a small village nestled in the foothills of the Fagaras Mountains which are the highest mountains in the Southern Carpathians. The taxi refused to travel any farther than that, citing the road conditions, or lack thereof, as the reason. The village lay in the shadow of a giant Citadel that loomed above them like some sinister guardian. The ruling families had once lived in the Citadel; way up high where they could look upon their people, and somewhere below, closer to the actual base of the mountain was the remains of the small village of the guardians.

Hiring a donkey cart to take her to the Inn was not an easy task. The roads were long and winding, and nobody wanted to be out on them after dark. The people were a superstitious lot, and their fear of the dark was tantamount to a terror Alicia understood completely. Alicia loved the night, the scent of night blooming roses, the chirping of the crickets, the peeping of the tree frogs as they called for a mate, even the buzz of the hungry mosquito was music to her ears. She loved the night. What she hated was the long dark hours when she slept, and was vulnerable to the *Seeker*.

Finally she found a farmer willing to take her along with him. He had a small farm just a few miles past the Inn, he told her, and would be happy for the company.

The journey was pleasant enough with the farmer regaling her with tales of the past in the mountains, while the cart bounced over the pothole-ridden dirt road that wound its way along the mountain pass. They travelled for miles along the winding road, sometimes with the mountains so close she could reach out and touch them; other stretches ran through valleys, and forests. The farmer made several stops at farms along the way dropping off supplies he had picked up in the village. Alicia got used to the farmers looking at her curiously, although not one questioned her presence.

The road wound its way through a forest with the trees so dense they blocked the sun. Alicia had the feeling that someone was watching them as they wound their way along the trail. The farmer clicked his tongue to encourage the donkey to move faster, and as if the donkey didn't want to be in the woods any more than they did, the cart bounced along the road. There were only a couple of hours before sunset when they finally reached the Inn, but the farmer ensured Alicia that he would make it to his own home in plenty of time before dark.

Alicia was entranced with her first view of the inn. An old cedar rail fence surrounded it and the immaculate gardens. A gate stood open to a crushed stone walkway leading to the two-story building. The back of the inn faced the mountain, but Alicia could see that the lower deck, as well as the upper balcony, both ran the full length of the outer wall, plus wrapped around both ends. There were several potted plants hanging from the upper balcony, their blossoms a riot of color against the darkened wood.

Across from the wooden gate, on the other side of the road was a flat area with the grass cut short. There was a large "Parking" sign with an arrow pointing to the grassy spot on the side of the road, not that it looked like there had ever been a car parked there. Alicia could not imagine too many drivers either brave enough, or stupid enough, to attempt to drive their vehicles down the so-called road.

The Inn was quiet when Alicia arrived; the only sound that of a child's laughter. She smiled at a young American mother and her two-year-old daughter, as the child chased the bubbles her mother blew for her. The mother was in her early thirties, with long straight black hair, and wide green eyes. The little girl had short curly hair, a shade lighter than her mother's, but the same wide green eyes. Their laughter drifted over to her, and Alicia sighed. She would never have a child of her own. There would be no curly-haired little girl chasing bubbles, or dark-haired little boy catching frogs.

Alicia climbed down from the cart, thanked the farmer when he handed her bag to her, and watched as he disappeared around a bend in the road. *Let's hope there's room at the Inn,* she thought, and walked up the path. The farmer did say that several of the archeologists were camping at the site. She smiled at the mother and child.

"Hi," the mother said. "I'm Molly, and this is my daughter Megan." She indicated the little girl who had taken up shelter behind her mother's leg.

" Alicia." Alicia smiled at the little girl, and held her hand out to her. "How are you, Megan," she said.

"Hi," Megan said from her safe spot behind her mother.

Molly glanced at the duffle bag Alicia was carrying. "Have you come to join the dig?" she asked. "Mike, that's my husband, didn't tell me they were expecting anyone else."

"That's because they aren't expecting me. Until this morning, I wasn't sure I was coming here."

The front door of the Inn opened, and a short, plump woman on the far side of sixty stepped out, wiping her hands on the apron she wore. " Welcome," she said, her accent making her W sound like a V. "I am Magda, welcome to our Inn. Pietro come out here. We have a guest."

An elderly man wearing baggy brown trousers, a white shirt, and a woolen vest rushed out the door, and grabbed Alicia's duffel bag. When he smiled there was a gap between his two front teeth.

" Show our guest to her room, Pietro," Magda said. She reached into the pocket of her apron, and pulled out a cookie which she gave to Megan. "Take her bags to number fourteen."

"You're right beside us," Molly said. " We have thirteen."

Alicia checked into the Inn, had a quick wash, and within the hour arrived at the dig. Professor Raven was thrilled to have Alicia on the site, although he regretfully informed her that they had no funds to hire her.

" Don't worry about it," she assured him. "I am actually on vacation, and was hoping that you would allow me to join you as a volunteer for a while."

"That we can manage," the professor told her happily. A student shouted excitedly, and the professor all but forgot Alicia in his haste to witness the new discovery.

Alicia was wandering around the dig when the buzzing started in her head. The further from the actual site she got, the louder the buzzing, until she was about a half mile away from where they were digging. Suddenly the buzzing stopped, and her vision blurred before it became very clear.

Screams rent the air. The ground below her feet ran crimson. Headless bodies littered the ground. A young couple, barely out of their teens, led a small group of children from the carnage. Even the smallest of the children was helping to carry the babies, as they disappeared into the surrounding forest. In the unearthly silence that followed the massacre, the village burned to the ground, and the remaining bones scattered in the wind.

These were her father's people. Alicia understood why it was so important to keep their presence a secret. People hadn't changed much over the years, they were still afraid of what they did not understand. She took several, calming breaths. Although they were not digging anywhere near this area right now, she vowed to do whatever was necessary to ensure that they never did. She would not allow those bones to be dug up, and proof that Lycans existed be found.

What could she do? She would be dead in a couple of months.

You do not need to die. Come to me.

The words were harsh with emotion, the guttural Egyptian accent evident. Even if she knew how to go to him, would she dare? Could she dare? Or, would going to him lead her right into another nightmare of her own making?

It must be your decision, little one. I will not force you. There was overwhelming sadness, and resignation in the voice. *I will stay with you to the end. You will not be alone.*

Alicia spent every day at the dig. Sometimes she would grab a brush and work alongside the other interns, slowly, painstakingly uncovering old relics. So far, they had only uncovered a few trinkets, and the tools of humans, but

25

Professor Raven was optimistic that they had found the ancient village of the protectors. The supernatural race of beings rumored to have protected the ruling families by turning into wolves to fight their opponents. A trail led from the spot they were digging, up the side of the mountain to the Citadel which towered above them, convincing Professor Raven that he was digging in the right spot. Alicia was not about to tell him any differently. It was his lifelong dream to find proof of their existence, and Alicia meant to do everything in her power to ensure that his dream did not come true.

~~~

Alicia was bone weary, and her face smudged with dirt where she continuously wiped away the sweat that ran steadily from her brow. The rubber band that held her hair had loosened, and several curly strands tickled her nose. She brushed them away, smearing another streak of dirt across her cheek. She didn't care. There was no room for a prima donna on an archeological dig. It was hard, meticulous work, and even the cooler, wet temperatures did nothing to ease her discomfort. Alicia looked around her at the other smudged grinning faces, and could not stop her own returning grin. They had uncovered their first bones today, and spirits were definitely high.

Professor Raven had personally supervised the careful extraction and packaging of the bones. They would send the bones to the University of Leicester for identification and carbon dating, and then Professor Raven would find out what Alicia already knew. They were simple canine bones. The bones were those of a wild dog that had starved to death. Nothing more—nothing less.

It was dusk when Alicia trudged the four miles to the Inn with a male intern who spent the entire time flirting outrageously with her. He was taller than Alicia by several inches, which didn't necessarily make him a tall man, and even with his dirty blond hair plastered to his face he was good looking, in a frat boy kind of way. For the past week he had found every excuse possible to be near Alicia, and she was beginning to find it rather annoying.

"At least have a drink with me before dinner," he pleaded.

There was a sudden lightshow in front of Alicia's eyes, and her head began to throb. Hunger clawed at her insides like a wild beast trying to claw itself from its prison. Her teeth exploded in her mouth. Stepping closer to her companion, she leaned into his throat. The naked fear in his blue eyes made her wet at her core, as she sank her fangs into his common carotid that carried the hot, fresh blood from his heart.

Swallowing the rising horror, Alicia shook the image from her mind, brushed a wayward lock from in front of her eyes, and forced a laugh she did not feel. " Before dinner I am going to have a warm bath." The water at the Inn was never warm, but it would help erase the horrid image of her drinking from his vein from her mind. "Then I am going to do something with this mop of mine, and change into something more comfortable."

Her companion did nothing to disguise the blatant desire that flared in his eyes. "You look fine to me," he drawled. "More than fine."

Of course I do. I'm absolutely gorgeous covered in dirt, and wearing an old filthy rain slicker.

A sudden crash of thunder made them both jump. Alicia looked up into the clear blue sky, very different from the dark clouds that threatened rain in the early morning, and this time she did laugh. Her guardian angel was at it again. Too bad he couldn't protect her from her own horrifying thoughts.

"Nonetheless, I think I will stick to my original plans and pass on that drink."

When her companion pouted, she could not help but tease. "Don't look so sad. We can still sit together at dinner." Sit was about all she could manage these days. It was getting more difficult each day to hide the fact that she was barely eating, and everything she did force herself to eat just came back up once she was in the privacy of her room. Liquids were about all she could stomach, and even those were beginning to cause her problems. Just the thought of forcing herself to eat something in front of these people had her stomach churning. *Or was it hunger that churned?*

"Right. You, me, and an Inn full of people." The more people the easier it would be to hide the fact she was barely eating. Besides, the last thing she wanted was to encourage a relationship with this, or any man. It would not be fair, not only did she not have the time for a long-term relationship, but the man held no more appeal to her than her brothers did.

A fleeting memory of one of her more disastrous dates flickered through her thoughts, and she sighed. A week, a month, a lifetime. It didn't matter how long she had. She had long since resigned herself to the truth that she would never find a flesh and blood man who could even remotely compare to the man of her dreams.

They rounded a bend in the road, and the Inn came into view. The young American mother, Molly, was again blowing bubbles for little Megan to chase while they waited for her husband to return from the site. Megan saw Alicia and forgot about the bubble she was chasing. "Lisa, Lisa," she called in her baby voice. The baby ran towards her as fast as her chubby little legs would carry her, with her arms stretched out in front.

Alicia smiled at the chubby girl, and waved. "Hello Molly," she called to the mother. "Mike asked me to tell you that he will be about an hour or so still. They are bagging bones."

"Eew. You make it sound so gruesome." Molly laughed. " Come here, Megan," she called to her daughter, who continued on her way ignoring her mother. " Alicia will see us at supper."

" Right supper," Alicia's companion muttered, and stalked towards the Inn without even trying to disguise his rancor.

Megan was about half the way between her mother and Alicia, when Alicia heard the rumbling.

Do not move. They can't see you if you don't move.

The wind roared like a freight train barreling down the tracks, straight for them. Alicia stared in horror as the massive ebony coach pulled by its two mammoth black bears burst through the clouds. *They can't see you if you do not move.* She prayed for divine intervention as she watched death coming for her.

The bears stopped, and snuffled the air. They couldn't find her. She was safe.

There was movement to her left. Terror gripped her throat, as little Megan ran straight for her. The bears turned as one, and sped straight toward the little girl.

Do not move. Do not move. Do not move. Even as the words ran through her mind, Alicia leapt toward the child.

She snatched the startled child into her arms, and stumbled, rolling as she fell to protect the child with her own body. Coming to a sudden stop, she sat up with the whimpering child tucked safely against her chest.

Thunder roared in her ears, as the bears' hot breath brushed her cheek. Megan whimpered. Alicia knew if they stayed where they were Megan would die. She couldn't live with the death of another innocent on her conscience.

There was a flicker of movement in her peripheral vision.

He stood there; Tall, Egyptian, and wearing only a loincloth that did nothing to disguise his manhood. His tanned body rippled with muscles, and flames flickered from the golden sun tattooed on his broad chest. His eyes locked with hers, and she stopped breathing. Heat pooled at her center, and her blood ran hot. Alicia melted beneath the radiating heat of those golden orbs. He silently offered his hand.

Alicia's eyes flickered to the fluttering nostrils of the giant bear, and back to the nearly naked god.

Three

There was a complete absence of light. She was standing in a fog so thick she couldn't see her hand in front of her face. The thick fog distorted the sound of their beating hearts, and their rapid breathing. Alicia drew in a deep breath, and slowly exhaled in an attempt to still the rapidly growing panic. Megan squirmed in her arms, and Alicia lifted her up so she was resting against her shoulder. "It's okay, sweetheart. Alicia can't see either." She gently rocked the child, murmuring sweet platitudes that helped to calm both her and the child, while she considered what to do.

The child does not belong here.

Shivers trailed down her spine at the deep timber of the familiar voice. She prayed her legs would hold her and

Megan upright. "Who are you?" she whispered, even now afraid to open her mind completely to him.

You know who I am little one.

She did know him. At least, she knew his voice. This was her guardian angel. She swallowed the lump in her throat, and whispered. "Where are we?" She had to know if the sound would penetrate the deep fog.

This is simply a passage between two places. The child does not belong here.

Alicia clutched Megan closer. *I will not allow you to harm this child. I will not be responsible for any more death.*

You misunderstand, little one. No harm will come to the child.

Alicia wanted to believe him. Every fiber of her being screamed the truth of his words. Megan did not belong here. She was a child with her entire life before her.

There was a sudden bright light, and the mist cleared slightly. He was so close she could smell his musky male scent. His blood called to hers, making her own blood burn, and her teeth ached for a taste. Alicia stared. She couldn't stop herself. He was without a doubt the most magnificent male specimen she had ever laid eyes on. When he moved, the muscles on his arms rippled, sending heat straight to her core.

See for yourself. He made a wiping motion, and the fabric of the universe opened giving her a window to the Inn. The usually immaculate garden was a disaster, the plants torn and tossed. Mike and Molly stood in the center of the chaos. Alicia was surprised to see the stubble of a beard on Mike's usually clean-shaven chin. There hadn't even been a hint of five o'clock shadow when she left him at the site barely an hour ago. Mike had his arm around his wife's shoulder, and he seemed to be helping her stand.

"Why aren't they looking?" Molly's voice was thick with tears.

"They have been looking for three days, Molly. They are not here."

Molly put her face in her hands muffling her voice, but Alicia heard every word as easily as if she were inside the other woman's head. "I know what I saw, Mike. I can't believe it, but I saw it. How can I convince anyone else when I cannot believe my own eyes?"

They walked to the exact spot where Alicia had stumbled with Megan. "Megan was running to meet Alicia." Molly sniffed, and swiped at her nose. " She loved Alicia because she always treated her kindly, even when she was so tired I thought she would drop where she stood." Molly sniffed again. " All of a sudden the sky darkened, and the wind began to howl. Megan suddenly stopped running. She just stared at the sky like she was seeing something that couldn't really be there. Alicia was staring at the sky too. You should have seen the look of terror on her face. Before I knew what was happening Alicia ran over and grabbed Megan. She stumbled, and they both fell."

Molly's wide eyes pleaded with her husband. "It all happened so fast. One second they were sitting on the ground staring into the sky. The next, they were gone. Alicia reached toward the sky, and they simply vanished."

"It was a tornado, Molly. Alicia must have realized Megan was right in its path. She was trying to protect Megan."

A tornado? What is going on? Exactly how long have we been here, and where exactly is here? Are we dead? Am I dead? Is that why you said Megan doesn't belong here, because I am already dead, and she is still alive?

33

Deep, rumbling laughter sent delicious shivers down her spine, at the same time it sent anger coursing through her veins. Before Alicia could vent, the nearly naked man started to speak, and Alicia relaxed as the deep timbers of his voice soothed her anger. *You are not dead. You have been here three earth days, and it is time to send the child home.*

Megan chose that moment to squirm around, and she spotted her parents through the window. "Mommy! Daddy!" She squealed, and tried to wiggle free.

At five foot four, Alicia did not normally feel small but her guardian angel towered over them. He had to be six foot six at the very least. She watched warily when he knelt on one knee, bringing his face level with Megan. " Are you ready to go home, little one," he asked. Megan's head bobbed and wide green eyes so much like her mother's stared at the strange man. She reached one small hand towards his chiseled features, and touched his cheek. A small gasp escaped Alicia when his face began to glow, and then he passed his hand in front of Megan's small face, and her eyes glazed over. "It is best if you do not remember anything of this," he said gently.

He took the child from Alicia's suddenly limp arms. "Wait here," he said to Alicia, and stepped through the window. *Sure, why not? She didn't have anywhere to go anyway.*

Alicia watched as the tall Egyptian set Megan carefully on the ground, and once again wiped his hand over her face. His body shimmered, and disappeared. Megan ran towards her parents. "Mommy, Daddy," she called in her little girl voice.

Alicia watched the couple bend as a single unit, and clutch their child close. They were laughing and crying as they took turns hugging Megan, all the time running their hands over her arms and legs checking for injuries.

"Are you okay baby? Are you hurt? Where were you? Where is Alicia?"

Megan squirmed uncomfortably in her parents arms. "You hurt me," she whimpered, and they immediately loosened their hold. They did not relinquish her. They were afraid that if they let go she would disappear again.

Mike and Molly searched every inch of their daughter without finding a scratch on her. Not so much as a smudge of dirt marred the child. If they had not lived through the agony of the past three days, they would think she had just been out playing.

Finally convinced there was no serious injury to their daughter, they reluctantly gave in to her persistent wriggling, and set her on the ground, although Molly still refused to release her grip on the child's hand. Mike made a quick search of the area Megan had come from, but although the ground was soft, the only thing he could find were about ten feet of Megan's prints. She had appeared as suddenly and as mysteriously as she had vanished.

Mike knelt so he was eye level with his daughter. "Megan." Megan's innocent gaze met her father's serious one. " Do you know where Alicia is?"

Megan's curly locks bobbed and she turned so she was staring straight at Alicia. Mike followed the direction of his baby daughter's gaze, and saw only a few clouds in a very blue sky. With a puzzled look on his face he repeated, " Do you know where Alicia is?"

"Yes daddy. With the glowing man."

Four

"Forfeit," Jade purred, grinding against Luke's obvious erection.

"Oh yeah," Luke growled lifting his lower body, and Jade with it off the floor. "I agree to do anything you want." He lowered his lids, and wiggled suggestively. "What doth my lady desire?"

Jade sighed, and relaxed against her husband's hard chest. She reached up and ran her fingers through the straggly ends of his normally thick beard, and then she gave it a little tug, grinning triumphantly.

Shit. She wouldn't, Luke thought suddenly wary. He should have realized what she was up to. Jade had been after him to trim his beard for months now. He didn't particularly like his beard as long and straggly as it was, but he refused to trim it to prove a point; that he could grow it if he wanted to.

"Oh yeah," she laughed. Her warm breath kissed Luke's already heated skin, and he groaned. "Cut it off."

"What?" *That is so not what he was expecting.* With a growl, Luke flipped them over so he was looming above his wife. God he loved her. Had from the first time he saw her, walking toward him across the crowded room at that seedy bar almost eighteen years ago, all sex and woman. It just took his brain a little longer to realize what his body knew instinctively, and with every moment they spent together their bond only grew stronger.

He would kill for her. He would die for her. And yes, he would shave his beard for her. Right after he did something else for her.

Jade's lips twisted into the crooked grin he adored, and her amber eyes shone with love. "Are you trying to weasel out of our bet, husband." Her voice was husky with need.

"No way." He was so close he could taste her breath as it came out in small pants of anticipation. "A deal's a deal. I just have one thing I need to do first," he said, and captured those soft lips.

The door opened, and Gheorgès strode into the room. At seventeen he was tall, and already showing signs of the man he would soon become. His features were dark, with a hard quality about them that some people found extremely intimidating.

"Get a room," he said, and then laughed. "Man, anyone saw you two would think you were newlyweds."

Luke kissed his wife again, stood up, and offered his wife a hand, almost surprised when she actually accepted the offered hand, and rose to stand by his side. He adjusted his sweats, which did nothing to hide his massive erection, before turning to his son. "I see you finally made it. Wasn't our workout for two?" Luke glanced pointedly at the clock on the far wall. "It's now three."

Gheorgès shrugged. "Something came up," he said. "Besides, it looks like Mom was a better workout partner anyway."

Luke ran his fingers through his straggly beard, and frowned. Then he smiled at his wife. "More interesting that's for sure."

Jade laughed, and reached up to give her husband a kiss. She was a tall woman, but Luke still towered over her, making her feel small and feminine. She playfully tugged at his beard. "Don't forget our bargain," she said.

"Luke's eyes darkened, and he waggled his eyebrows in a *Snidely Whiplash* sort of way. "How about a rematch," he said. "All or nothing."

Jade gave her son a kiss on the cheek. "Don't worry," she said in a stage whisper. "I wore him out for you."

Gheorgès pointedly looked at the bulge in the front of his father's sweats. "Doesn't look like he's worn out to me." He didn't need to see the physical proof of his father's desire for his mother; he smelled it the moment his walked into the room.

Jade laughed again, and crossed the room. When she reached the door, she half turned back. "Completely off," she threw at her husband. "And a rematch would have the same result."

As the door closed behind her she heard her son's voice. "You're not really, right?"

"A deal is a deal," Luke said as the door clicked shut.

The moment Jade left the bottom level of the ranch house where their training area was, she felt that shift in the universe again. It was nothing she could pinpoint, but it was there just the same. Something big was coming. She only wished she knew what it was. Jade didn't like this not knowing, especially with Alicia out there somewhere on her own. Not for the first time, Jade cursed the restrictions on her own powers. As *Moarte* she knew when one of their laws had been broken, where the crime had been committed, and often found herself in the right place on a feeling that she was going to be needed. She sometimes wished she got the feeling before the crime was committed. The trouble was, until a crime was committed she had no authority. That didn't mean that when a crime was committed she automatically knew who the guilty party was. She didn't just swoop down, and exact justice, but she did have excellent tracking and investigative skills which she used to her advantage. In most cases the best witnesses to a crime were the victims themselves. All Jade had to do was find the body in time.

Right now the urge to go to Mexico was nearly overwhelming, so overwhelming in fact that she found her feet taking her to the telephone instead of the shower. She picked up the phone and dialed a number by rote. After a half dozen rings the other end picked up.

"O'Connor Search and Rescue, how may we help you?" The pretty voice belonged to Theresa, Matthew's mate.

"Hi, Theresa, is he around?" The *he* Jade referred to was Matthew. Matthew was *Lobo*, born a wolf with the ability to take on human form. His mother had died during childbirth, and his father had raised him in the forest far from human contact. Matthew had very little experience with humans until caught in one of their traps and his father died trying to rescue him. When Jade found him, he was in a cage at the Center for Physic Research, where they were doing secret experiments on him. Jade rescued him, and taught him how to embrace his human half, and how to control the magic he possessed as *Lobo*. Matthew soon became a trusted member of O'Connor Search and Rescue, the company founded by Jade's human father, Sean O'Connor.

Matthew had stayed at the Ranch, working with her father, training the search and rescue dogs when he wasn't on assignment with Jade, until Jade opened a division of O'Connor S&R in Mexico, and asked Matthew to stay there, and run it.

"Jade. How are you? Matthew is out on patrol. He's been edgy for about a week, but there hasn't even been one missing person's report let alone anything strange." There was a pause, and then, "Matthew wants to know what's happening."

Jade sent an image of herself rolling her eyes at Theresa. They were too far apart for her to have a private conversation with Matthew, but the open phone line helped her connection with Theresa. "Not one for small talk is he?"

Theresa's soft laughter tinkled over the open line. "I wouldn't exactly call you a master at chit chat. It's `hi Theresa is he around?' No, how are you? How's life? Any news you'd like to share?"

Jade cringed. That's exactly what she did. Luke would have asked all the usual questions before asking for Matthew, but Jade still had trouble getting too close to people. In her business it wasn't always a good idea, but that was no excuse for rudeness. Besides, she actually liked and trusted Theresa. She had from the moment she met her, and she was thankful that Matthew had found her when he did. "I'm sorry, Theresa. How are you, and Matthew?"

"We're good, Jade." Jade couldn't help but catch the hint of excitement in Theresa's voice, and wondered why she hadn't noted it before. " How are you, and the family?"

"Luke is shaving his beard off."

"No!"

"Today."

"I thought you liked his beard?"

"I do, but he decided to grow it long, and refused to trim it so I challenged him. Of course I won. I think he was looking for a way to save face. He doesn't like his beard long and straggly any more than I do, but it became one of those he couldn't cut it off without looking like he was giving in to me."

" But he is just trimming it, right?"

"No. I told him to shave it *all* off."

Theresa laughed. "You are so evil."

Jade snickered. "You should have seen the look on his face. It was worth all the whisker burns I'm going to get in retaliation when it starts to grow back in." " So are you going to tell me, or are you waiting for Matthew to say something?"

With a rush of excitement Theresa burst out. " We're pregnant."

Wow! Jade really was not expecting that bit of news. "That is great," she said. " When?"

" Six months. And don't worry, Jade. Matthew and I aren't quitting you."

" But..."

"No. We discussed it. We love this job. And it's not really that dangerous."

"Fighting vampires, and rogue werewolves isn't dangerous?"

Theresa sighed. "You know what I mean. I did agree to phone duty for the duration of the pregnancy, but not a moment more."

There was the sound of a door opening and closing, and then Matthew's voice. Jade could picture him giving his mate a kiss, and patting her belly, just from the muffled sounds that carried over the wire. "How you feeling?" "Tired?" " Hey Junior you being good for Mommy?" " We are so not calling him Junior." "We'll see," and then his voice got louder. "Jade. What's happening? I've been edgy all week, but I can't pinpoint the cause."

Before Jade could get a word in he continued. " Aren't you supposed to be in Willow Bend with the family?"

" What makes you think I'm not?"

"Telephone I.D. Call came in from the ranch. Ain't technology a hoot? What gives?"

" Alicia cancelled. Told Em something came up, and ever since I have been edgy myself. Can't seem to track her down."

" What can I do?"

It was a long shot, but Jade couldn't shake the feeling that she should be on her way to Mexico. " Can you check out the farm?"

The *farm* was the property of Alicia. She inherited it when her parents were murdered. The locals considered it cursed, although the official story of the Martinez family deaths was attack by a wild animal. Stories of the *Chupacabra* have been around for years, and the locals would believe what they chose to believe.

"Nobody's been around. I just came from there."

Jade was disappointed although she hadn't really expected anything different. It was just this feeling she had that would not go away. "Thanks, Matthew. Could you check again in a few days? I can't shake this feeling."

" Will do, Boss."

"Thanks. Oh, and Matthew."

"Yeah, Boss."

"You're going to make a great dad." Jade hung up before Matthew could respond.

Five

He was generating so much heat Alicia was sure she would burst into flames, and he wasn't touching her—yet. She wanted to lean back and let those flames devour her. She was tired of running. She was tired of the constant pain that made her head feel like it would explode. She was tired of the horrid hallucinations where she became the creature she dreaded the most.

Most of all she was tired of being alone. Just once she wanted to feel a man's arms around her, and actually *feel* something. Well something besides hunger which is all she ever seemed to feel these days.

The mist gathered, closing the window on Megan and her family. It was so quiet she could hear the beat of their hearts, and their irregular breathing. She nearly jumped when he broke the silence.

"So much for forgetting," he whispered the words close to her ear, the deep somber tones sending waves of desire coursing through her body, and need clenching at her womb.

What was wrong with her? She had never reacted to any man this way. In fact, she had never had any reaction to a man at all. What was it about his voice that made her want to rip her clothes off, and his? Not that he was wearing much. "I can't imagine it would be easy to forget being whisked away to...," Alicia indicated the surrounding mist with a flick of her wrist. "Where did you say we are? And while you're at it, who did you say you were?"

"This is merely a passageway."

"Hmm." Alicia chewed on her lower lip, and her eyes narrowed thoughtfully. She absently rubbed her forehead against the growing pain. "Where, exactly, does this passage lead?"

"Nowhere." His muscles rippled when he shrugged. "Everywhere."

Well, didn't that narrow things down a lot? Alicia felt his body stiffen, at the same time a tickle of unease began in her stomach. *Oh god, it was back. How had it found her here?* Alicia turned to warn the Egyptian, and had to shield her eyes. The tattoo on his chest was glowing blood red.

This time there was no hesitation on her part. Alicia placed her smaller hand in his much larger one, and closed her eyes against the wave of dizziness that enveloped her. When she opened her eyes she was standing in a large courtyard, completely surrounded by pyramids.

She blinked. They were still there.

Her right hand tingled, and she realized that *He* was still holding it. She gave it a small, reluctant tug, not really wanting him to relinquish his hold. He held on tighter.

The large stone door to one of the pyramids opened silently, and a man who was taller and broader, yet could be twin to the man holding her hand—right down to the sun glowing on his bare chest—strode toward them. The two men clasped forearms, before the taller man pulled the smaller one closer and clapped him on the back, ignoring the fact that he still held Alicia's hand firmly in his.

"Kamenwati," the new stranger boomed. *So that was her guardian angel's name.* "It is good to have you home." He stepped away from Kamenwati, and bowed low. "Welcome to our humble home, daughter of Alaric."

Home! Alicia gaped at the opulence of her surroundings, and the God who stood before her. This had to be another hallucination, although she had to admit it was a lot more pleasant than her usual ones.

She blinked, and the bronzed God remained before her— definitely the Egyptian Sun God Ra Horakhty. She would recognize his image anywhere. She should have seen the similarities in the man who held her hand. She probably would have if she weren't so distracted by the attraction she felt. Ra Horakhty was the reason she had worked so hard to be accepted on the Egyptian dig. She had to admit his pictures didn't do him justice. He was absolutely magnificent. It took Alicia several moments to process everything that was happening, and then it hit her. *Daughter.* "Hold on a minute. You must have me mistaken for someone else. I am Alicia Martinez Wulfson, adopted daughter of Luke Wulfson and Jade Caer. My real parents were killed when I was eight, and I have never heard of the Alaric."

"Alaric is Prince of the Magi." Kamenwati's deep, seductive tones threatened her sanity, and turned her knees to jelly. She was grateful her knees didn't buckle right then, and make a fool of her.

Me the daughter of a Prince, that's a laugh. "You definitely have the wrong girl."

Kamenwati heard her silent laughter, and his feelings for the slip of a woman whose hand he held made his tattoo settle into a steady golden glow. He had been watching over her for what at times felt like eternity, waiting for her to acknowledge his presence, understanding why she was terrified to do so.

Ra raised an eyebrow at his son. "So that's how it is." Ra's voice boomed in the stillness of the courtyard.

"Yes," Kamenwati answered. There was no sense in trying to hide anything from his father, and he was not ashamed of how he felt.

Alicia looked from one stoic face to the other, unable to read anything in either. "How what is?" she finally asked, but neither offered her any explanation.

The all too familiar tickle began in her stomach, and she was suddenly terrified as that glowing tattoo shifted from a soft golden glow to a blood red blaze. How had the *Seeker* followed her here? She tried harder to tug her hand from Kamenwati's, but he held it tight. "I have to go," she pleaded quietly. "Please, Kamenwati let me go."

Both men stared at her silently. Kamenwati held her hand a tiny bit tighter. *Do not fret, little one.* His deep voice enveloped her, giving her what she knew was a false sense of security.

It couldn't be real. She was not safe. Not as long as the evil hunted her. *Please, Kamenwati*, she begged silently. *Do not make me responsible for any more death.*

Kamenwati gave her hand what he hoped was a reassuring squeeze. *You were never responsible.*

The warning tickle in her stomach grew stronger, and Alicia grew frantic. She tugged her hand free, and stared at the two men with her hands on her hips. "What is wrong with you? *He* is close. Can't you feel it?"

Two pairs of golden globes stared at her as if she had suddenly grown two heads.

Fear and anger made her limbs tremble. "What is wrong with you," she demanded. "I need to leave here immediately. If *He* finds me I won't be able to save you."

Kamenwati reached out to take her shaking form in his arms, but she slapped at his hands and stepped aside, resisting the urge to just give in and allow him to protect her. She would not give in to her own desires, and delay leaving here any longer.

Go inside. The push was strong, and Kamenwati's step faltered.

You are safe, little one. His spirit voice surrounded her, caressed her, and made her want to believe.

Almost.

"I am not safe," she said loud enough for both men to hear. "I am not safe, and you are not safe. Not as long as I am here. I need to go—Now! Before *He* finds me again." Although she had never seen the creature inside the black coach, she instinctively knew it was male. She looked into Kamenwati's golden orbs, and her voice broke. "I can't let him hurt you." *Please,* she begged silently. *Don't let me hurt you.*

The taller Egyptian roared with laughter at the thought of a mere slip of a girl protecting his powerful son, and Alicia's blood began to boil. She turned to Ra then, her dark eyes blazing with fury as all rational thought fled. "This is not funny you Pompous Ass. This *thing* has been chasing me for years. I have lost everything once because of these creatures. I will not stand here and let that thing take anyone else from me."

His golden orbs sparking, the bronzed god held her in thrall. "Pompous ass? Me?" His voice was barely above a whisper, and yet it reverberated like thunder.

Alicia refused to let him to see how much his anger terrified her. So maybe she shouldn't have called him a pompous ass, but he was acting like one, even if he was a god.

I see you.

Sheer terror clutched her heart in its icy grip. It was too late. She had to get out of here—now! Before anyone else got hurt because of her. Her head began to throb, and her vision blurred. Power coursed through her body. When Kamenwati reached for her, instinct took over just as it had when she was two and chased by a very large dog. She threw her hands out to ward him off, and shock waves threw him off his feet. Out of the corner of her eye she saw Ra swing his arm towards her. She heard Kamenwati's "No!" at the same time the sparks flew from Ra's hand, and her whole world disappeared.

Six

The wheels of the custom built Cessna gently touched the tarmac, and the large plane rolled silently to a halt. Luke's voice came over the speaker as clearly as if he was standing in front of Jade. "You can let go of the armrests now," he said. " We have landed."

After nearly twenty-four hours of flying time, Jade was a wreck. It was no secret that she was terrified of flying in an airplane. "If Cerridwen wanted me to fly in a plane she would not have given me wings," she would say. Unfortunately great distances made it necessary to sometimes take to the skies by other than under her own steam. Besides, Luke and the boys couldn't take to the skies like her and Emerald. They were Lycan, and able to shift only to wolf form.

The Cessna had been custom built with over seven foot ceilings to accommodate the Lycans larger size, and each of the twelve seats not only had vast amounts of head and shoulder, and foot room, every one reclined for comfort on long flights. Along with the larger headroom, the plane had a full service galley, while the larger washroom had hot and cold running water for showers, and flushing toilets.

Emerald unsnapped her seatbelt just as Gheorgès and Luke stepped out of the cockpit. Luke insisted that they all knew how to pilot all their personal aircraft in case of an emergency, and that included this much larger plane. This trip Gheorgès was getting his first lesson on piloting the larger Cessna, which didn't bother Emerald in the least. She preferred to pilot the helicopters because she liked the view better.

Luke glanced over at Jade's bloodless fingers, her nails digging into the leather upholstery on the armrests, and sighed. "I guess you won't want a flying lesson anytime soon."

Jade laughed, and loosened her grip. "I fly quite well thank you," she replied. "I don't think I need any lessons." The family laughed at the familiar exchange, and Jade announced. "I'm starved." She never could eat on a plane.

There was another burst of laughter. Quinn reached into his jacket pocket, and pulled out a chocolate bar which Jade grabbed, and had unwrapped in the blink of an eye. Her love for chocolate was as legendary as her fear of flying.

Daniel Dixon came out of the cockpit, the flight book and a pen in hand. "Hey Boss," he said, scribbling something on the paper. "I will get this bird fueled up, and ready to go at your command. I'll bring on supplies if I can get any here. We need fruit and veggies, gas, water, the usual." Daniel Dixon was not only a trusted employee and friend, he was also family, the official pilot, and chauffeur, etc. Daniel glanced up from his paper and winked at Jade. "There's roast beef sandwiches in the fridge. I wouldn't let this hungry mob eat it all on you."

Ten minutes later they were through customs, and Daniel had already started to refuel and restock. The airport was small but Luke had called ahead to ensure they would be able to get what was needed to continue their journey.

The moment they stepped out of the airport they were aware of the curious looks from the few locals who were out and about at this time of day. Not many tourists came to this part of the Carpathians, and those who did flew in on the regular weekly flight. Five strangers arriving in the middle of the week by private plane were bound to generate a lot of curiosity.

Jade smiled at an old woman wearing an ankle length black skirt, and a colorful top. "Hello," she said. " We were …"

Before she could ask directions to the archeological dig they had traced Alicia to, the woman made the sign of the cross in front of her chest, and hurried across the road muttering to herself. Jade glanced over her should to see Gheorgès and Luke glaring after the woman, while Quinn seemed as surprised as she was.

" What do you suppose that was about?" asked Quinn.

" Gheorgès scared her," Emerald said, a hint of laughter in her voice. Emerald narrowed her amber eyes at her brother. At seventeen he was already six foot tall, and where at fifteen he had been all skin and bones, now he was packing on some well developed muscle. With his straight dark coffee hair, and ebony eyes he should have been gorgeous but his penetrating looks, and almost permanent scowl made him appear too intimidating to be handsome. Top that off with his black T-shirt, and black leather pants, both tight enough to show off every one of those well-developed muscles when he moved, and the knee-high black motorcycle boots he preferred, and he was downright scary. Emerald asked him once why he dressed to intimidate, and his answer was "If they are scared they won't pick a fight." It made sense, but Emerald still liked her brother better when he wasn't trying to be intimidating.

Gheorgès scowled at his sister who laughed aloud, and Quinn rolled his eyes at the pair of them. "I'm serious," Emerald finally said. "She thinks he is the *vârcolac*, and I don't blame her. When he scowls like that he scares me, and I love him."

"You made that up," Gheorgès growled. "And what is this *vârcolac* supposed to be anyway?"

"Werewolf." Luke's voice was barely above a whisper, but they all heard it loud and clear with their super hearing.

Emerald's amber eyes widened with shock. "You're kidding, right Dad?"

"No." Luke adjusted the pack he had to both shoulders, and strode down the street his own dark features twisted into a scowl. He ignored the few people that actually turned to watch his progress. "Let's go," he growled. "We're burning daylight."

Jade shrugged her own pack into a more comfortable position, and fell into step beside her husband. She was used to being shunned, or feared, but it rankled that a stranger's passing thought had the power to hurt her mate.

I know where she would have gone. Luke sent his wife a mental grimace. *It was superstitious villagers like her that destroyed my family and home not far from here. There is an archeologist up the road that is trying to find evidence that my race exists. That's all we need, irrefutable proof that Lycans exist.*

Luke was born in these mountains, in a small village nestled in the foothills beside the Olt River. His race were the protectors of the ruling family until a group of villagers afraid of the *vârcolac* banded together and tried to massacre every last one of them. Luke watched while they murdered his mother, his baby brother in her arms, before he managed to escape with a small band of children. They made their way to the new world where they settled in what was now Willow Bend, Canada.

Luke shoved the painful memories from his childhood back where they belonged, in the past, and the moment he rounded a bend in the road hiding them from prying eyes he shifted into a large grey wolf. Within a heartbeat there were two white wolves, two grey wolves, and a large black wolf standing in the middle of the dirt path that passed for a road.

With a growl, the leader took off into the woods knowing that the others would follow. An hour later the pack stopped at the edge of a clearing. Voices drifted toward them on the breeze, and they lifted their noses to taste the air. In a blink of an eye the wolves were gone, leaving the Wulfson family unit standing in their stead.

She's not here. Jade sent the thought to her husband.

We will find her. Luke's voice was husky over the private link he shared with his mate. The group waited for instructions, not wanting to bring attention to their selves. *It will be better if we don't all show up,* he said on the common path he shared with the rest of the family.

Quinn eyed his brother's dark countenance, and strode towards the clearing before anyone could object. *I'll go.* "Hi." He smiled at the two teenage girls nearest to him. They were carefully dusting off some old piece of pottery while chatting about someone named Steve. His voice must have startled them because they jumped, almost knocking over the fragile piece, and turned to face him. They were both dressed in dusty denims and t-shirts, but that is where the similarity ended. The girl closest to him was tall, about five foot six with long blonde hair that was trying its best to escape the rubber band she had it gathered in, to frame her round face.

She stared at Quinn with pale blue eyes, and her mouth slightly open, but no words came out. The other girl was shorter, no more than five foot one with short curly red hair, a pale heart shaped face speckled with freckles, and flashing green eyes.

Those green eyes took in every aspect of his appearance; the dark coffee colored hair that covered his ears and curled at the nape of his neck, the ebony eyes that stared without blinking, the knowing smirk on his handsome face. His white button up shirt was open at the top revealing a small medallion with a wolf etched on it nestled at the vee against his bronzed skin. The white shirt tucked into the waist of comfortably worn blue jeans, and he wore brown hiking boots. There was paint under his fingertips. When she looked back at his face, his smirk grew as if he were laughing at her.

Her green eyes flashed. "Who are you?" she demanded, eyeing his backpack suspiciously.

I would love to paint you, Quinn thought. *Those flashing green eyes full of fire and subtle strength. That fiery hair and those freckles. God I could kiss those freckles.*

Concentrate baby brother. Gheorgès voice growled through his mind, and Quinn mentally rolled his eyes throwing the image at his brother. "Well I haven't come to steal your relics," he said, adoring the way the female blushed. "I am supposed to meet with my sister. Perhaps you know her, Alicia Wulf, uh, Martinez." For a moment Quinn forgot to use Alicia's professional name.

The redhead still eyed him warily while the blonde suddenly came alive. "Oh. You are Miss Martinez's brother? She didn't tell us she had any brothers. Then again, Miss Martinez doesn't talk about a whole lot unless it has to do with the dig. She is a very quiet person."

Unlike you once you get going. Quinn's lips parted showing a row of straight white teeth. " Do you know where I can find Alicia?"

"Miss Martinez isn't here today. She was staying at the Inn down the road, but nobody has seen her or Mike for...," she glanced at the redhead but didn't wait for an answer. "What has it been, three days?" She paused when she realized the redhead was glaring at her. "Uh, anyway, she was staying at the Inn down the road. It's about two miles down the road."

Quinn pointed toward the only road. " Which way?"

The redhead eyed him with even more suspicion, as if that were possible. "You must have passed it on your way. It's the only place between here and town."

"Oh, *that* Inn." Quinn flashed his brilliant smile at the girls again, grateful to see the redhead blush. "I probably should have asked there on the way by, but my sister usually stays on site," he lied.

He could feel those green eyes burning into his back until he rounded a bend. He wasn't surprised to find his family there waiting for him.

Seven

She was tumbling head over heels as silent gray mists swirled around her. She should have been trembling with fear, instead her heart rejoiced. "Find me now you bastard," she screamed, and began to laugh hysterically. She was free. Ra had killed her, and by doing so had saved his son.

Her guardian angel.

Her soul.

As suddenly as it appeared the mist disappeared, and Alicia landed with a thump on the hard ground. Dust flew up and tickled her nose. She sneezed. Her butt hurt where it connected with the hard surface.

"So maybe I'm not dead." The sound of her own voice echoed eerily in the silence making her wince worse than the pain in her backside. Alicia stood up and checked herself for broken limbs before brushing the dust from her clothes. Not that it helped much. She was still wearing the same dusty clothes she had been wearing at the dig. She shielded her eyes from the bright sunshine, and peered around cautiously. The churning in her stomach had ceased, confirming that she was alone—for now.

Alicia took a few moments to get her bearings, wished she had thought to bring her sunglasses when she had left the Inn this morning, and then she began to laugh hysterically. During the short time she and Megan had been in the twilight zone three days had passed on earth. She had no way of knowing how many days had passed in the time since then. A sense of loss so strong it nearly brought her to her knees enveloped Alicia at the mere thought of Kamenwati. She wiped the tears from her eyes, snuffled, hiccupped, and forced herself to calm down. She thought longingly of her sunglasses sitting on her dresser back at the Inn, and suddenly they were covering her eyes. Alicia grabbed the glasses, and stared at them. They were definitely her glasses. There was a small scratch on the left lens from when she dropped them on the ground last week.

Then it struck her. Her head didn't feel like it was going to explode at any moment. She had better take advantage of the reprieve, and find shelter quick. Alicia placed her glasses over her eyes, and studied her surroundings.

The air was hot and dry. The vegetation was scarce, some cacti and shrub brush which reminded her of Mexico. Her heart started to pound with excitement, and she took a closer look at the surrounding yucca and mesquite. Her head began to buzz, low at first and then louder, and stronger as the murmur of voices urged her toward the low ridge of mountains to her left.

Four hours later, hot, thirsty, and exhausted Alicia stared at the little stone cabin where she had spent most of her childhood. Some of the boards that covered the windows were cracked, and others had rotted away completely. The building was in obvious need of repair, and felt deserted. Still she hesitated before approaching to reach out with her senses, and listen. The house was empty. The barn, what was left of it, was also empty. There were a few wild chickens strutting around in the yard, but other than them, the farm was completely deserted.

Still, Alicia approached the house cautiously and peered through a broken board on one of the windows before going back and pushing open the front door. She staggered under the onslaught of emotions that assailed her. There were no living residents in her old home, but that did not mean it was completely empty.

The door to her bedroom was hanging on its hinges, and she thought she saw a shadow glide past the opening. She moved silently, drawn by an unseen force to the bedroom. Across the room under the boarded up window sat the hand carved bed she had slept in as a child. Her favorite toy, a monkey her mom had made for her from a pair of her Papa's old woolen socks sat on the floor at the foot of the bed. She loved that sock monkey when she was a baby, and it slept on her pillow every night as a little girl.

She sat on the bed and clutched the monkey tightly, ignoring the bugs that made their home in its stuffing. Her vision blurred, and she was no longer in her bedroom, instead she was in the room she shared with her parents in their old house.

Alicia sat with her chubby legs crossed, one hand holding the bar of the handmade crib. Her other arm was stretched out through the bars, reaching for the half-emptied bottle of milk setting on the cupboard top. "Bottle," her baby voice said in her native tongue. The bottle wobbled, and then straightened itself. "Bottle," she said more forcefully. This time the bottle wobbled, but instead of steadying itself it rose from the cupboard top, and drifted toward the crib. Alicia's small fingers wrapped themselves around the bottle as soon as it was near enough, and with a satisfied grin on her face she popped the bottle into her mouth.

Her mother came into the room, and rushed over to the crib. She took the bottle from her daughter, and scolded. "You cannot just take whatever you want, Alicia. It is not safe. You must wait to get things like a normal person."

Alicia's baby self did not understand the words her mother said, but she had no trouble understanding the tone. She began to sob. Her mother lifted her out of the crib, and held her close rocking her.

"I'm sorry, little one," she crooned. "I did not mean to upset you. I just want you to be safe."

Her Mama's voice soothed her, and she closed her eyes. When she fell asleep, her mother laid her in her crib, carefully tucked the blankets around her, and tucked her sock monkey in beside her. "You must learn to hide what you are, and what you can do," she whispered to the sleeping child.

"What am I, Mama," she whispered into the silence of the empty room. "When do I quit hiding?"

Alicia walked on leaden feet to her parents' bedroom. She loved this bed as much as her own. She often came into her parent's room in the middle of the night after a bad dream, and crawled between them. She would go back to sleep then, knowing she was safe with her parents to protect her.

The howl of a coyote broke the silence, and a shiver ran down her spine. She sat on the edge of her parents' bed, closed her eyes, and let the images of the past wash over her.

She was barely two when it really hit him. She was not his daughter. She held his heart and soul in the palm of her tiny hand. He would give his life for her without hesitation. She called him Papa, but he did not father her. His genes did not make her different—make her special. When she scrunched up her tiny, round face so much like her mother's, and reached for a toy just out of reach it would float through the air until she could wrap her chubby little fingers around it. She did not get that from him—and her mother did not do those things. That was the legacy from her true father.

He could not love her any more if she had been of his seed. The moment he laid eyes on his Maria, the most beautiful woman he had ever laid eyes on, bravely facing the world around her while pregnant and alone, he was lost. Her beauty drew him to her; her courage and determination captured his heart. She could have a dozen children, and he would love them all because they were a part of her.

It was hard to hide Alicia's difference from others. He would never forget the day they had fled to this place. The neighbor's dog chased her. She was running with her tears streaming down her cheeks when she suddenly stopped. Everything happened in slow motion, yet not slow enough that he could stop it. She turned, threw her arms out in a protective fashion, and the dog went flying through the air. Accusations of witchcraft travelled quickly amongst the superstitious people of their small village. That night they barely escaped with their lives when their neighbors burned their home to the ground in an attempt to rid themselves of the witch.

Gilardo Martinez took his young wife, and baby daughter, and brought them here to his family's farm.

She was five when she first realized she was different from other children, and that she was the reason they didn't venture into town very often. Not that they needed to. Almost everything they had was here on this farm. They raised goats for milk, and chickens for meat and eggs. Her Mama's garden was small, but she managed to charm the soil into providing them with enough to support their needs, with a little left over to take to market. Papa was an excellent woodcarver and he not only made the furniture in their home, he made furniture for others as well. They kept to themselves most of the time, only going to town about once a month to the local market where they sold eggs, milk, and homemade cheese. Maria had a reputation for making the best cheese in the area, and sometimes people would come out to the farm looking to buy some. They also sold fruit from the small orchard her mother coaxed from the dry earth.

Alicia was happy on the farm. It was her job to feed the chickens and collect the eggs. She would pretend it was a game, distracting the hens while she made their eggs float into her basket. Alicia was happy, but she was a little girl, and sometimes she felt lonely. Sometimes at night, she sat on her bed and wished for someone just like her. A girl who could hear people's thoughts, move objects with her mind, and would be her friend.

What she got was a monster.

Alicia gasped, and her eyes flew open. Her heart was thumping, and her breath came in rapid gulps. Poor Papa. Poor Mama. They had died because she was lonely.

Alicia swiped a tear from her eye, adjusted her sunglasses, and walked out into the yard. A couple of chickens scratched and pecked at the dry earth. They were either offspring of their own chickens, or had escaped from a nearby farm. Although there were no flowers in view, the sweet scent of morning glory filled the air. A grackle whistled from its perch on top of the barn. The cicadas droned merrily in the background, all completely unaware of the ghosts that lived on this small farm.

Her stomach growled, and Alicia tore a leaf from an Aloe plant. She broke the skin, peeled it, and bit into the slimy fruit. Someone had boarded up the windows in an attempt to keep the animals from encroaching on the house, probably Matthew, Jade's man, or rather wolf, in Mexico. Alicia appreciated his thoughtfulness. She would have to look him up and thank him, but the boards gave the farm a deserted feeling that saddened her.

She was not going to leave the farm like this. Her mother had loved this farm. She had coaxed tiny saplings into mature fruit trees despite the dry soil, and even now Alicia could see those trees struggling to survive in the orchard beside the house. She had made this simple dwelling into a home anyone would be proud of, a haven of sunshine, laughter, and love. Alicia was not going to let her mother's life have no meaning. Just because her own children would never play on the old wooden swing in the yard, climb the trees in the orchard, feed the chickens, or collect the eggs didn't mean that no child would. She would turn this farm back into a place anyone would be happy to call home, and then she would put it up for sale, if she had the time. Oh well, if she did not get it done it wouldn't be for lack of trying.

With more determination than strength, Alicia tackled the boards on the windows. Lucky for her, most of them were already loose, and some had actually fallen off. Still, by the time she had finished her nails were torn and bloody. Now that there was more light in the small house, Alicia went in search of something to use to clean.

She found the broom, or rather what was left of it, in the cupboard behind the wood stove in the kitchen. The handle was still in one piece, but the bristles had either fallen out, or been pulled out, perhaps to make a bed for some rodent. Determined to finish what she had started, Alicia headed for the old barn.

She lifted the bar that held the doors shut, and set it against the wall. The doors opened a lot easier than she anticipated. Their sudden movement startled a flock of bats from their roosting place under the rafters. They darted at her a couple of times before settling back down. The interior of the barn was dark and damp. Over the smell of stale hay and mold Alicia detected dried animal feces, and the scent of blood making her wonder what else had made its home in the old barn.

Ignoring the bats, she grabbed a handful of straw from one of the lofts. Alicia bent the straw over, and then used some wire she found in her Papa's old workroom to fasten it to the broom handle, surprised that nobody had ransacked the barn before now. Satisfied with her makeshift broom she returned to the house, and swept all of the rooms.

Now that the thick layer of dust was, if not actually gone, moved around a lot she realized that the house definitely needed soap and water. Alicia leaned over the deep well in the front yard. It was too dark to see the bottom, but she could definitely *smell* water. She dropped a pebble from the yard, and listened for the kerr-plunk as the pebble hit the surface of the water. Satisfied she would get water, she grabbed the long handle to wind up the water bucket, frowning at the sound of falling water with every turn. *This can't be good.* The wooden bucket that hung from the old rope was missing some slats, and by the time it reached the top it was empty.

This required another trip to the barn where Alicia found an old tin bucket. The handle was missing, but she used some more wire from the workroom, and made her own handle. Armed with water from the well, and an old hunk of lye soap she was lucky enough to find in a cupboard in the kitchen, Alicia set out to remove every trace of dirt from her family's home.

Alicia pulled out the bottom drawer of her mother's dresser, and an old yellowed envelope fell to the floor. She set the drawer to the side, and picked up the envelope. The moment she touched the paper she felt her mother's arms wrapped around her, making her safe. Her mother's voice whispered in her ear, words of love and encouragement, as she had in life. Alicia sat on the bed, and turned the envelope to read the writing on the front that was in her mother's handwriting. *Why had Mama felt the need to write this letter so long ago?*

Alicia Martinez

To be opened on your 21st birthday.

Alicia turned the envelope over several times, squeezing it with her fingers. It felt several papers thick, and there was a hard bulge in one corner. With shaking fingers she carefully opened the envelope, and pulled out the carefully folded papers. She ignored the small gold chain that fell out, her eyes glued to the familiar slant of her mother's handwriting.

My darling Alicia

This is the hardest letter I have ever written, because if you are reading this I have not survived to your twenty first birthday.

I have started this letter a hundred times, and even now I am not sure how to say it, so I am going to just come right out with it.

You are Bruja.

You come from a long line of Bruja. *You were born with psychic abilities, as were all the females in our line, although none have displayed these abilities at such an early age. I fear that has something to do with who your father is.*

Let me tell you a bit about our line so you might understand some of your powers. I received the Gift of Earth. I encourage things to grow in the most barren of places. The proof of this is my beloved orchard. My mother, your grandmother received the Gift of Voice. She could hear thoughts, and speak to others with her mind. I have never seen proof of you speaking in this way. You have never reached out to Papa or me but I know you can hear our thoughts. Your great grandmother had the Gift of Movement, the ability to move things with her mind. This also I have witnessed in you. We can all cast minor spells, although I very seldom call on this ability as there is always a price to pay. It is rare for any Bruja *to receive more than one gift, but you have always been special and I have seen the signs even while you were very young. Before your second birthday you were already displaying a rare amount of power, and I know that one day you will grow into a very powerful* Bruja.*

Do not be afraid.

Embrace your Gifts. To try to deny them can be quite painful. One day you shall pass them to your own daughter, as they have passed to you.

Your papa, Gilardo Martinez, is a fine, proud man. He loves us very much, as we love him. He has been a wonderful papa for you. I met him at a time when I was once again alone and scared, and this time very pregnant. He never asked about the man who fathered you. Not even after you began to demonstrate your amazing abilities. He never asked, and I never volunteered the information. It was not that I wished to keep this information secret but every time I start to tell him about your father my memories grow fuzzy, and I am unable to utter a word.

I would not say anything now except I made a promise to your birth father, and I am afraid that if I do not put this in a letter I might not be able to fulfill my promise. His name was Rick, and he came to me in the night. I was sixteen when I met him. I was alone. I had just buried my mother, and he was strong, kind, and oh so handsome.

I do not remember much about my own father. I remember his coming home from the fields, dirty and tired, and always with a smile and a kiss for Mama and me. He died of the fever when I was five. Poor Mama was heartbroken, but she struggled to make a life for the two of us. It was not until I was thirteen that I received my Gift. We were beginning to think I had been passed over, it sometimes happens in a generation although rarely.

How I wish it had come sooner. I could have helped poor Mama coax a living for us from the earth, and maybe she would not have given so soon. Maybe she missed my papa so much that she could not wait to join him again. I prefer to think that this is true. I hate to think she gave up on life, and me.

If you are reading this letter, I have already gone to join with Mama and Papa. I know there is no proof, but I believe that when we leave this life we move on to another with those that have gone before us. Please tell your Papa, my beloved Gilardo, that I am anxiously awaiting his arrival. Not too anxiously. I wish him a long and happy life. I will wait forever if that is how long it takes him to join me. Alicia hoped they had finally found each other again in the afterlife.

You are probably wondering about the pendant. Alicia barely glanced at the pendant before continuing the letter. *It belonged to your birth father. His name is Rick, and he came to me in the night when I needed him the most. Poor Mama caught the fever the winter I was fifteen. It was a long, hard winter and she joined Papa the day after my sixteenth birthday. It was almost as if she was afraid to go before then. The day I buried her I was heartbroken.*

Rick came to me that night. He was so handsome I could not resist him. He stayed for nearly a month, making those long nights bearable. He taught me I could survive without Mama. He helped make me strong again. And he made me happy. I thought I loved him, until I found my wonderful Gilardo.

I do not know what to tell you about your father. He was wild and handsome, and very powerful. He could do the most amazing things. This I remember now, which is very strange because whenever I think about Rick, those nights, or the things he could do my memories become very hazy. My only clear memory is the night he left me—left us. It was early, barely dusk when he came that night. It was the first night of the three moons, and I was thinking how lovely it was going to be walking in the path of the full moon with the man I loved at my side. Rick was very anxious that night and it made me afraid.

Rick took this pendant from around his neck where he always wore it and he slipped it over my head. I remember how my chest burned when the pendant touched my bare skin.

"Give this to our daughter," he said. I thought he was going to cry, and I felt tears in my own eyes. I knew then that he would not be coming back.

"I will," I told him. My own voice was shaky with the tears that I was trying so hard not to shed. I didn't know how he knew about you. I was planning to tell him the night he left.

"Promise me," Rick repeated. He grabbed my arms then. I remember that he was holding me so tight that it hurt. His eyes went black and I felt like I was falling into an abyss. "On our daughter's twenty first birthday you will give her this pendant."

All I could do was nod. I had no voice. Even now while I write this letter I can feel his words burning into my mind. "Give it to our daughter. Tell her to put it on, and call my name. Alaric."

No, that cannot be right because your father's name is Rick. My beautiful Rick. Still the name he said to say was Alaric. I can hear his voice as clearly today as the day he spoke those words. "Tell her to put it on, and call my name. Alaric." He definitely said, Alaric.

The pendant has power. Too much power for me, but I know you will be able to handle it. Your own power grows each day. I can see it. Embrace your destiny, Alicia. Do not be afraid of who you are.

Do not be afraid of the pendant.

I love you

Be happy

Mama

Alicia picked up the pendant from where it lay on the bed. It was a miniature golden sun, set inside a cage of the thinnest golden strands, and hung from a fine golden chain. It looked so delicate Alicia was surprised that it had not crumbled with time.

Her palm began to itch, and her vision blurred. The room disappeared, and she saw herself in a graveyard kneeling beside a freshly dug grave. Alicia knew instinctively this was her mother as a young girl. Her face streaked with dried tears, and her eyes were puffy and swollen. Alicia drifted towards her mother where she floated above her for a moment before she pulled into her mother's body with a snap. For the first time in her life, Alicia was not seeing a vision, she was living one. She was her mother, seeing through her mother's eyes, thinking her mother's thoughts, and experiencing her mother's feelings.

Night rolled in like a steamroller blanketing her and everything else in darkness. Her knees were beginning to ache from kneeling so long on the cold, hard ground, but Maria didn't notice. She didn't notice much of anything these days.

For months she looked after Mama while she lay abed burning up with the fever, and now she did not know what to do. She had tried so hard to keep happy thoughts while she bathed her mother's weakening body, but Mama knew how scared she was. Maria could see the knowledge in her dark eyes, as Mama fought so gallantly not to succumb to the fever, not once complaining. Now there was no reason to hide her fear, no reason to pretend.

She didn't hear his approach, but she felt his presence, and she turned towards him. His dark eyes rimmed in gold, and his full lips parted to show straight white teeth. Her heart skipped a beat, and Maria wasn't sure if it was fear, or the man himself that caused the reaction. When he offered his hand she willingly placed herself into his care.

The vision changed, and Alicia was no longer looking at the stranger, but she was the stranger, see her mother through his eyes the way she was at sixteen, young, alone, and vulnerable.

The way she was looking at him with those dark, troubled eyes, her every emotion flickering to the surface, fear, curiosity, and above all the pain. Her pain cut him like a knife inflicting a wound so deep he thought it would suck the very life from his soul. What was it about this slip of a female that drew him, made him feel her pain? The way her eyes dipped down in the corners with the weight of her emotions gave her an exotic look that he found very sexy. He wondered what she would look like with a smile on those full lips, and happiness sparkling in her eyes. Even tired, with dirt on her knees, and her hair sticking out awkwardly from the severe roll she had pinned it into she was so beautiful she astounded him. He couldn't wait to sink himself deep inside her while he tasted her divine nectar. The spicy power rushing through her veins teased him. His fangs began to elongate even as he felt the first stirrings in his groin. He licked his lips in anticipation, the need to taste her urging him forward.

Alicia gasped, and dropped the pendant onto the bed as if it were on fire. "You bastard," she hissed into the approaching night. " She was my mother."

Eight

Alaric paced the black marble floor of his throne room without seeing the beauty of the candles reflected on the polished stone surface. The sounds of cascading water from the waterfall in the center of the vast room did nothing to soothe his anxiety.

Where was she? The nearest he could pinpoint was somewhere in the north of Mexico. That made sense. He had met her mother in Mexico, his sweet Maria. It had broke his heart to leave her on earth when he returned to his duties as Prince of the Magi, but although she was not completely human, she was not Mage and she could not have survived for long in his world, as he could not have survived in hers. As Prince of his people he had a powerful enemy, one that would gladly destroy his sweet Maria to get to him. No, it had been better to leave her behind.

At least that is what he kept telling himself.

Where was she? Why had she not come to him? Where was Conall?

With a thought, the huge cast iron bell at the end of the room began to clang, the two massive oak doors silently opened, and a tall lanky redhead strode into his chambers. He wore straight legged blue jeans tucked into cowboy boots, a buttoned shirt, opened at the neck and rolled to the elbows, a cowboy hat, and the gun belt and holster he wore slung low over his hips wasn't just for show. The man had been a Texas Ranger in the 1800s before his transformation, and was an excellent shot. The guns sitting in the holsters had special bullets, and he was quite capable of throwing the knife he wore tucked into his boot.

"You wanted me, Sire?"

Alaric cringed. He hated it when the man called him Sire. He was not this man's father, but he refused to rise to the bait today. "Where is Conall? I *requested* his presence in my chambers." Every mage knew that a request from the Prince was tantamount to an order.

Tex loved to rile his Prince, but he also knew the signs well enough to know when not to push. "Conall has been cooling his heels in the anti-chamber for the past six chimes," the redhead said. Time in their realm did not pass the same as on earth. Their days were long, measured in chimes rather than hours, and equivalent to roughly thirty earth days. Their nights were much shorter, coinciding with the three nights of the earth's full moon.

"Why was he not brought in immediately he arrived?" Alaric almost spit the words, and forced himself to take a deep breath to help him calm down.

Tex mentally rolled his eyes. Something was definitely up with his Prince. The man simply did not get distracted this close to nightfall. "You said to have him wait until you called for him. I'll bring him in now."

Tex strode through the massive doors, returning before they had time to close completely accompanied by a bear of a man. At six foot six, Conall was a good four inches taller than Tex; he was built like a warrior, with eyes as flat as frying pans.

Conall knelt on one knee before his Prince, his long black coat billowing out behind him, and laid his sword at Alaric's feet. "My Liege," he said. "My will is yours. My life is yours."

"Rise Conall." Alaric had no time for formalities today. "Leave us," he ordered Tex.

Conall rose, sheathed his sword, and cocked his head at his old friend. He was dressed in black leather pants tucked into motorcycle boots, a black t-shirt, and his favorite black duster. With his black hair tied behind his head with a leather bind, and his obsidian eyes boring into him, Alaric found it easy to see why his fellow Magi referred to him as the Fighting Irish, or the Black Irish. The second the massive oak doors clicked shut behind Tex, Conall said, "You look like hell."

Alaric shrugged. "I feel like hell." He hesitated for only a heartbeat, and then blurted. "I need you to go to earth."

"Now? Are you insane?"

"Don't be impudent, my old friend," snapped Alaric. "And yes, now. If I wanted you to go tomorrow I would have sent you tomorrow."

Conall was not the least bit intimated by his Prince. "Who am I going for this time?" was all he said. One of the things that Alaric trusted him to do was find human descendants of the Magi who were about to make their transition. Depending on the outcome he would bring them into the *Chimera*.

"My daughter."

"Daughter?" Conall squeaked.

77

Nine

Kamenwati picked himself up off the ground, and glared at his father. "Why?"

Ra's golden orbs glittered dangerously, but Kamenwati ignored the warning. "What have you done?" he growled.

Ra flicked his wrist, throwing his son back onto the dusty ground, and strode into his home. How dare that little chit come between his son and him; his own flesh and blood? Kamenwati had never spoken such to him. Perhaps he should not have sent the girl away, but she had threatened his son, and that he would *not* tolerate from anyone. Besides, she would be a lot safer on earth than she would be here when night fell in a couple of hours. At least that was what he tried to convince himself, knowing she would not be safe on earth during the early days of her transition. The

Betrayer had reached her once, and he would reach her again.

His footsteps were silent as he strode across the vast marble chamber, and approached the throne room. Throne room what a joke. He had not felt like King of anything in more centuries than he cared to remember. There was a time when he was King of all he surveyed, a God, worshipped by man. Now the only bright spot in his sterile existence was his son, and it looked like he was about to lose him to a mere chit of a girl.

Ra Horakhty sat upon the high backed chair made of solid rock, and took a moment to survey the vast chamber. The onyx walls reflected the emptiness of his existence. This room was quiet. Too quiet. What it needed was the patter of little feet, and the laughter of children; his grandchildren.

Ra felt a slight stirring of the air around him, and Kamenwati stood before him. His golden eyes still blazed with barely contained rage, but he never said a word. Ra sighed. "This isn't a home. It's a tomb."

Kamenwati lifted one brow slightly.

"I sometimes wonder if I was a little hasty when I left earth."

"You think?" Kamenwati's voice dripped with sarcasm.

Ra snapped his fingers, and a large wooden chair fitted with comfortable cushions appeared behind Kamenwati. "Quit your posturing and sit down Kamenwati. We need to come up with a plan."

"I need to go to Earth." Kamenwati sat stiffly in the chair. It was a small rebellion, but he was satisfied with the slight frown on his father's face.

"You know that is impossible. You will break the seal."

"The seal is broken." Kamenwati ran his hands through his golden tresses, and tried to still the sense of urgency he felt. *Where are you, little one?* She was blocking him from her mind, and it hurt so much he could hardly breathe. She thought she was protecting him from the evil that hunted her, but she was not. He faced that evil every setting of their sun, along with his father and the Magi.

"The girl?"

" She has a name." Fear, and a need like he had never experienced before made his voice sharp.

Ra glanced up at the ceiling, which was a colorful depiction of his last days on earth. A reminder of what he left behind, and what they fought at the end of every rising. He had it done so he would never forget that even his most trusted friend could betray him.

His enemies had stormed his temple intent on destroying it, and him. These were his Magi. Mortal men he had bestowed with the powers of the Gods. The Mage who led his enemies was once a High Priest, a man he should have been able to trust like a brother, the second mortal to ever drink from the *Ankh*. Not satisfied with the powers he already had, the Mage lusted for more. After several days of battle, and many deaths, Ra managed to ensnare his betrayer with magic. He cast him out into the void between the Heavens and the Earth, and then in a fit of rage Ra Horakhty cursed those who worshiped *The Betrayer* and their descendents to walk forever in darkness. He gathered his loyal Magi, and gave them the option of staying on earth or joining him beyond the Heavens.

Ra returned to the *Chimera*, and sealed it from the earth. Only those who possessed a key could traverse across the seal, and visit both worlds.

When he left, Ra took the *Ankh,* the Well of Eternal Life, with him into the Chimera forcing the Magi who chose to remain on earth and continue the battle against the vampire to drink blood to survive. Some tried to survive on the blood of animals, but human blood was more powerful, and the blood of a human possessed of magic was very powerful. Blood born of magic was a beacon in the night, calling to both predator and prey, and those who possessed it were always a target.

Vampires were those who forsake the sun to follow Theron in his evil quest to rule the world, and those who remained faithful to Ra remained able to walk in the day. These are the Children of Ra–Magi. The offspring of the union between a Mage and a human were born with unique and sometimes very powerful gifts. By the time they reached their early twenties food alone could not sustain their bodies, and they were forced to seek blood to survive. *The Betrayer* searched for these newly transitioned Magi in an attempt to turn them to the dark side. When they drained their victims, it released magic into the universe that the Betrayer could use to enhance his own. If the newly transitioned Magi chose not to listen to the urgings of the Betrayer, he simply sent those who did to destroy the Magi, thereby releasing their magic back into the universe for him to claim. As far as the Betrayer was concerned, it was a win-win situation.

Still, there were those who were strong enough to resist the *Betrayer*, and avoid the attempts on their lives, instead becoming part of the army that hunted the vampire. The Magi were not alone in their fight against the vampire, but still their numbers increased, and *The Betrayer* grew stronger.

Although the girl, Alicia, was not responsible for the seal being broken, she was in danger from *The Betrayer*. Until she accepted who she was, she was a threat to them all. Her power was strong, stronger even than that of her father. Ra knew why the *Betrayer* had chosen her. With her power, he would be able to remain on the human realm.

Darkness was falling in the *Chimera*, and they had to prepare for the worst. The seal was broken, and that meant the Betrayer would probably take this battle to Earth where his followers would be at their strongest, during the full moon. If he did, it could mean disaster for them all.

"You might want to prepare," Ra told his son. "You are going to Earth."

Ten

Two white owls silently landed in the branches of a great pine. Their wide amber eyes took in the mess of the yard and garden, in stark contrast to the well kept Inn with its wrap-around porch, and top deck. A small female child accepted the fussing of her parents with barely any squirming. Emotions ran wild in this small group of humans. Relief. Love. Fear. Grief.

The smaller owl on the limb beside her shuddered and Jade wrapped her in a feeling of warmth, and protection. As if they were reading each other's thoughts they drifted to the ground below, and shifted to human form.

Mike turned at the sound of cart wheels and hoofs, and watched the two strangers walk through the open gate. They both wore t-shirts, one blue the other grass green, well worn snug fitting denim jeans and they carried identical back packs. One woman was tall and lithe with short cropped white blonde hair streaked with strands of silver and gold. The other was about five foot tall with the same white blonde streaked with silver and gold, only her hair hung to her waist. It was their identical amber eyes that captivated him. He had never seen anything like them.

"Hello." Jade smiled at the man, and turned her attention to the woman and child. "Hi. I'm Jade," she said. " And this is my daughter Emerald."

My God, thought Molly. *They look more like sisters. I hope I look that good when Megan is that old.* Molly realized she was staring at the pair with a dopey expression on her face. "Uh, hi," she finally stammered. "I'm Molly." She lifted the squirming child into her arms, and held her close. "This is my daughter, Megan." Molly glanced furtively toward her husband who was still staring at the newcomers with a strange dazed look. "That's my husband, Mike. Mike. Say hello," she prompted.

"Hello," he said.

Molly narrowed her eyes until her forehead puckered, looking first at her husband, and then at Jade and Emerald. She squeezed Megan tight enough that Megan yelped, and tried to wiggle out of her mother's arms. " What brings you to this part of Romania?"

" We are looking for my other daughter. We were told she was staying at this Inn."

Molly ran through the guests at the Inn. It didn't take her long. Besides her family there was the newlywed couple from Brisbane, Antonio, Marcus, and Steve who left right after Alicia disappeared. *Poor Alicia. God she hoped she was alright.* Molly could think of nobody who looked remotely like these two. Molly neared dropped Megan when Jade said. "Her name is Alicia."

"Lisa," Megan squeaked, and wriggled harder. "I want to see Lisa."

" Shh baby," Molly crooned. " We all want to see Alicia."

A wolf howled in the distance, and Mike stepped closer to his wife and daughter, his eyes clearer. "Take Megan inside," he ordered Molly. He offered his hand in greeting to Jade, who shook it, but she couldn't read him at all. "I'm Mike. I was working with Alicia at the dig before she disappeared. Maybe you better come inside where we can talk."

" Disappeared." Emerald's voice was a whisper of pain.

Another wolf howled sending shivers through Mike. "Let's go inside. Magda will be happy for the company."

The door to the Inn opened to the main dining room. There were two long picnic tables on the left built out of logs, and were sturdy enough to hold twenty large men easily. There was a bar on the right made of pine, with four tall stools, and a mirrored back board that made the entire place appear doubled in size. An ancient woman came rushing through the swinging door at the end of the bar, wiping her hands on the apron that protected her black skirt. Her long sleeve white shirt was somewhat covered by the slightly embroidered leather vest she wore. Hot on her heels was a shorter man wearing baggy brown trousers, a white shirt, and a woolen vest. His grin revealed a missing tooth.

" Welcome back, Miss Megan." The woman spoke with a thick accent. Her sparkling eyes smiled at Molly. "I told you Miss Megan would be returned safely."

"Yes you did Magda. I am so glad you were right." She squeezed Megan who yelped. Laughing, Molly set her on the floor, comfortable now they were safely indoors. "You stay right where I can see you," she warned her daughter, who was already heading toward Pietro. "I don't want you to get lost again."

"I wasn't lost." Megan pouted at her mother. "I was with Lisa."

Emerald dropped her pack to the floor, and knelt in front of Megan locking her amber eyes with the child's wide brown ones. "Did you and Alicia get lost?" she asked in a quiet, compelling voice.

Megan shook her head until her curls bobbed crazily. Emerald lifted one eye brow slightly. Molly and Mike felt the urge to pick up their child, but neither could move. It was as if they were frozen in place.

"We weren't lost," insisted Megan, her small voice growing thrill. "We were with the glowing man. He saved us."

For a heartbeat the room was so silent you could hear a pin drop. The door exploded in and three very large men stroke in. The two wearing jeans and button down shirts were scary enough, but the large one wearing black leathers and motorcycle boots was absolutely terrifying. Molly moved then, with a frightened gasp she snatched up Megan, and ran for the stairs beside the kitchen door.

Quinn calmly picked up his sister's pack, and helped her to her feet. Luke walked over, put his arm around his wife, and kissed her on the cheek, nodding to the Inn keepers in silent acknowledgement. Gheorgès scowled, and strode toward the staircase, stopping suddenly when Mike jumped in front of him.

Gheorgès glared at the human who was half his weight, and a good eight inches shorter, but the man held his ground. The smell of his fear was acid in Gheorgès' nose, and Gheorgès was surprised to find he was impressed with the human who dared stand between him and his prey.

They are not prey, admonished Jade. *They are humans who have just been through a very traumatic experience.*

Gheorgès nodded to the human barrier. "Forgive me," he said his voice a soft growl.

Mike sagged against the railing in relief when he realized the huge male was not going to pursue his family. Meanwhile, Magda seemed completely oblivious to what was happening around her. Her full attention was on Luke. Suddenly her dark eyes widened, and she whispered in Romani Carpathian. "Lykos."

Luke's head whipped around, and his gaze locked with the woman's. "You are mistaken," he growled in the same language.

Magda hurried over to the wall on the other side of the picnic tables, and removed a picture from the wall. When she returned she shoved it into Luke's hand. Luke's hand trembled when he looked down at the photograph. It was a very old black and white photograph, and it was a photo of his family. His father was smiling, and he had his arm around Luke's mother. Even in the ancient, grainy photo you could see the love in her eyes as she gazed upon the face of the infant she held in her arms. Luke was standing beside his sister Helen. He remembered when they took this photograph. He was sixteen, his sister Helen was five, and Gheorgès was only a couple months old. His father warned them about the dangers of capturing their images on film, but his mother had wanted the picture.

Luke's eyes burned, and his throat ached with unshed tears. This was his family two years before the massacre that took the lives of his beloved parents, and nearly his entire pack. The massacre he was responsible for. He sent Jade a mental smile when she squeezed his fingers. Her love poured over him like a security blanket. *I love you.* They sent the thought at the same time.

Luke swallowed painfully, and looked up to see everyone in the room staring at him. The room hummed with power. The human male looked confused. There were tears in

Emerald's eyes, and Quinn was holding her while her body trembled. Emerald was already a strong empath, and she was experiencing Luke's feelings. She was still learning how to control her ability but was having difficulty being in such close proximity. It was slightly easier with strangers and only then if her mother was near enough to be her buffer.

Dad? Her spirit voice was wet with tears. His tears.

My family. He made an effort to get his emotions under control, and was relieved when Emerald's body quit shaking.

Magda's dark eyes flickered from father to daughter, and she sighed with satisfaction. It was true then. Everything that passed from generation to generation was true. The Protectors did exist. They were still out there. She stepped closer to Luke, and tapped his image on the painting. " This is you," she continued to speak in the old Romani Carpathian dialect so the human would not understand.

I nearly killed him to deny them, but Luke handed the grainy photograph back to her. " I don't know these people." He didn't realize he had answered in the old language, until Magda grinned, and nodded her head.

The Innkeeper looked at him as if she was looking straight into his soul, and pursed her lips. "The young." She tipped her head toward the three siblings now standing together. The two males flanking their sister. "The young might like to see their elders." She tapped the image of Luke's father. "Your father left his photograph with my people with instructions to give it to you when you returned." She locked eyes with Luke, but he managed not to show her how much she unnerved him. "That photo has been on that wall for centuries waiting for you. Are you going to deny your own family?"

She is telling the truth. Your father gave the photo to the original Innkeepers. He knew you would come here one day, and he wanted you to have something to remember the good times. Did your father have the gift of prescience?

I remember when he had this taken. He forbade everyone to let the photographer capture their images. When mother said she wished she could have something to look at when we were not together anymore, Father got this strange look on his face, and suddenly gave in. He said `it will give him something to remember us by.' God. Did he know then that they were going to die?

Your father wanted you to have that picture, Lykos. Take it.

Luke thanked Magda, and carefully put the picture in his pack, before turning toward the human male. "We are going to need to speak with your daughter."

Mike's spine stiffened, and he grew taller. "I'm not going to allow you to scare my daughter."

Jade patted Luke on the arm, and stepped between the men. Her amber eyes locked with Mike's, and she smiled. "We are not going to scare Megan," she said in a soft, hypnotic tone. "We need to ask her about Alicia. She will not be frightened, I promise you."

Mike's head nodded slowly, and he didn't even try to stop his wife and daughter from coming down the stairs.

Jade knelt in front of Megan so she was level with the girls wide green eyes. "Orange eyes," Megan said.

"Yes I do. And you have beautiful green eyes. Like your mother's."

"Lisa eyes brown." *I like Lisa. I want to see Lisa.*

Jade reached out and took the child's hands in hers. There was an almost audible hum in the room, as Jade's power focused, and she saw what happened.

Eleven

The room grew dark as the sun faded behind the mountains. Still Alicia could see the room as if it were noon. The sounds of the night sang to her. The buzzing of a mosquito as it searched for its dinner, the scuttling of small rodents in the dry grasses, the huu-huuu of an owl. The walls of the small room seemed to be closing in on her. Alicia wanted to leave the pendant where it lay but her hand snaked out and picked it up. Although she fought the urge to do so Alicia slipped the pendant over her head, and walked out into the night.

A million stars twinkled against the black velvet backdrop of the night sky. A bat flew past her head, and a wolf howled in the distance. Hunger beat at her. She needed to go to the nearest village to get something to eat.

There was a rush of air around her, and Alicia found herself standing on the edge of town. A wave of dizziness hit her, and she fell to her knees gasping for air until it passed.

You need to feed.

Hunger brought her to her feet, and carried her forward. Her legs moved on their own without her knowing where she was going or what she was going to do when she got there. She moved through the night like a shadow, silent and dangerous. Alicia wanted to stop, to turn around and go back to the safety of the farm, but something forced her to keep moving forward. She felt like a puppet on a string, and it terrified her.

The night breeze carried the scent of jasmine and moon vine, the overpowering stench of dead fish, and human sweat. She was in a fishing village she had visited as a child.

Alicia crinkled her nose in distaste, and stepped from the shadows. Hunger was a wild beast clawing at her insides, urging her forward.

She needed to feed. *No. I need to eat.*

She rounded a corner, and the scent of male and blood assailed her. Her womb coiled in anticipation, and her fangs lengthened until they pressed against her lower lip. She followed the scent silently, a predator of the night. Desire and hunger at war within her, all thoughts of retreat gone.

He was alone on the pier. His muscles rippled as he loaded the heavy boxes into the cart. His heart beat steadily, pushing warm, delicious blood through his veins. The coppery scent made her mouth water.

Call to him.

The need was too strong to ignore. *Come to me*, she called out to the human with her mind, and the spicy scent of desire filled the air. The male tilted his head as if listening, and he sniffed the air. He dropped the heavy box he was holding, and it broke on the surface of the pier spilling its contents.

His hazel eyes searched the shadows until he spotted the dark alley. He shuffled toward her, one foot in front of the other like a zombie. He struggled to halt his progress, afraid of whatever hid in the shadows. Compulsion carried him forward.

Fangs exploded inside her mouth, and her tongue slipped over the tips tasting the yellow liquid that dripped from them. The male was near enough she could see the stark terror in his eyes, and still his legs carried him forward. He was less than a foot in front of her when he stopped. His eyes glazed over but his thoughts screamed for him to stop, to escape while he could. It was already too late. Terror raced through his veins making his blood more potent.

The male tilted his head to one side offering her his throat, his blood, his life. Her fangs grew longer, and hunger clawed at her urging her to feed. She leaned into his neck. The call of his blood a compulsion she could no longer ignore. The tips of her fangs touched his skin and his fear was pungent. The tips of her fangs pierced his skin.

An image of her Papa standing before the beautiful monster made her stomach clench in distaste, and horror. *No,* her mind screamed.

Alicia shoved the male away. *Run.* The compulsion was strong, and the man stumbled in his haste to flee. Alicia fell to her knees as exhaustion overwhelmed her.

You need to feed.

I will not feed. I will not become the monster that killed my family. I will die first.

Then you will die.

Twelve

The girl was strong, the *Seeker* would give her that, but she was no match for him. Already the hunger ate at her soul, and her refusal to embrace her fate made her weak.

It made no difference to him if she lived or died. Either way he would control her power.

Thirteen

Kamenwati reached out to the fleeing man's mind, filling it with false memory.

A noise startled him, and he dropped the box he was holding spilling coconuts everywhere. Ignoring them he listened to the night. There was something at the end of the alley. Cautiously he peered into the darkened alley, but he could see nothing except the outline of a dumpster. He was about to turn back when there was a loud screech, and something jumped out of the shadows. He ducked, but he was not fast enough. Its outstretched claws caught the side of his neck. Shaken, but relieved it was nothing more than a cat, he returned to the pier to clean up the scattered coconuts.

Satisfied that the man would remember nothing more than a run-in with a stray cat Kamenwati gently lifted

Alicia's trembling body as if she were a mere child. Compared to him, she was. An infant in a world she could barely fathom, who possessed more courage in her soul than the most courageous warriors he knew.

With a mere thought he opened a doorway, and stepped through to the small stone cabin she once called home. Kamenwati laid her on the single bed, instinctively knowing she would be unable to rest in the bed where her parents had once slept. He held her in his strong arms until her trembling ceased. Kamenwati's hand moved of its own accord, gently sweeping the hair from her face; his eyes feasting on her beauty. His heart constricted in his chest. He wanted nothing more than to lean into her and taste those blood red lips. As if she could read his mind her eyelids fluttered, and the look he saw in those dark eyes made his pulse race.

Kamenwati swallowed. "Go to sleep, little one," he whispered, his voice husky with desire.

"Stay with me." Her own voice was thick with desire, and her eyes were huge in her pale face.

"I'm not going anywhere," Kamenwati promised.

Alicia shifted to the far side of the bed, even that small amount of effort nearly proved too much for her. She laid her hand on the empty space beside her. *Please. I don't want to be alone. I'm afraid.* She was tired. Too tired to talk anymore, too tired to fight anymore, and she did not want to die alone.

You are not going to die, little one. Kamenwati lay on the small bed beside her, and gathered her tightly against him. She seemed very tiny against his much larger form. Alicia sighed, and her breath caressed his bare chest. *I have waited too long for you. I refuse to let you go.*

Safe in his arms, Alicia closed her eyes.

Fourteen

Jade sat in a small clearing surrounded by tall pines, and majestic firs. She felt so small, so helpless. It wasn't a feeling she had often, and she damned well didn't like it. Her daughter, her first child, was out there alone somewhere, and Jade didn't know how to find her.

Of all her children Alicia was the one she worried about the most. Alicia was strong and powerful with her own special gifts, but Jade could never completely forget the first time she saw her. She was laying on that flat rock surrounded by trees, a sacrificial lamb with a vampire leaning over her. Her power shimmered in the air above her, a calling card for the monsters who craved her. Her silent sobs were daggers in Jade's chest. Jade wanted to protect her then—as she wanted to protect her today.

Where are you Alicia? She cried out to the surrounding night.

When no answer was forthcoming, she turned to the heavens. *Blessed Cerridwen. Goddess of Inspiration. Goddess of Knowledge. Bestower of thine gifts upon my unworthy soul. I need your inspiration and guidance now more than ever. Please show me the way.*

The compulsion to go to Mexico intensified. She was not going to be able to ignore it much longer. There was a power base building there. A shift in the universe that was unlike anything Jade had ever experienced. She tried to ignore it.

Sometimes our paths take us where we most need to be.

Quick on the heels of that thought was an image, flickering like an old black and white movie on a cracked screen. There was a tear in the universe, and a man stepped through. He was well over six feet tall, with the build and stance of a warrior. He reminded her of Gheorgès in black leathers, and black motorcycle boots, only this man wore a leather duster that flared out behind him giving her a glimpse of the weapons he carried. Jade tore her vision from the man, and studied the surrounding terrain. The sparse vegetation consisted mostly of cactus and scrub brush.

It looks like I'm going to Mexico.

~~

Conall stepped through the portal, and froze. There were eyes on him. His eyes tracked his surroundings without uncovering their hiding place. His nostrils flared. He was alone, but that didn't lull him into thinking he had not been seen. Someone had watched his entrance to earth, and that meant he had to work fast to find the prince's daughter before someone else did. The air around him vibrated with power, and the portal closed.

Damn you Alaric. What in hell had his prince been thinking? Slumming on earth—procreating. He knew better than most the dangers of a mating between a Mage and a human. He knew the risks involved. But he was Conall's prince, and as such it was not Conall's place to question him.

Conall's nostrils flared once more as he sensed the air around him. The air was rife with power fighting for release. A faint glow on the horizon beckoned him. Conall prayed he was not too late, and strode toward the source of power.

Fifteen

Death was coming for her. She could smell its rotting breath on the night breeze. Alicia did not fear death. It would be a welcome release to step into death's embrace and escape the hounding of the *Seeker* with his glistening black coach, and those ferocious black beasts that hauled it.

Death wasn't supposed to be like this. She thought she would simply go to sleep and not wake up.

The fire started deep inside her belly, and quickly became an inferno burning her from the inside out. Her blood was already beginning to bubble in her veins, and it felt like they would burst to let the steaming fluid escape. Pain stabbed at her belly. Her body went rigid, and then doubled over onto itself as the scream escaped her lips.

Flames engulfed her, burned into her brain. She held her breath to keep from searing the delicate tissue of her lungs.

Breathe little one. Kamenwati's voice washed over her like a spray of cold water and her skin began to sizzle.

She gasped, and began to pant, trying to work through the pain. Her clothing was melting against her skin. She had to get it off. Alicia started to tear at her clothes with nails that had grown into claws not even noticing that she tore her own skin. The coppery scent of blood wafted in the air. Her nostrils flared and her fangs elongated. Another wave of pain ripped through her veins tearing another scream from her already torn throat. Her body stiffened.

Breathe baby. You keep forgetting to breathe.

It was hard to keep the panic from his voice. Kamenwati had never witnessed a human's transition to Mage. It was terrifying to watch. He knew the risks. Not every Mage was strong enough to walk through the fires of the universe, and not all those who did survived with their minds intact, never mind their bodies. Kamenwati could understand why so many went insane, forgetting they were ever human, and embracing the dark. He felt the fire burning through her, attempting to burn her memories away one by one so she could be reborn. He was trying desperately to hold the link with her, to help her through this, but he was afraid it might not be enough. What was the good in being a God if you couldn't help the one you loved?

Loved? Hell, when had that happened. Kamenwati had been watching over Alicia since she was a child, impressed by her bravery in the face of so much pain and heartbreak. He had heard her silent cries, felt her power, and it drew him to her, as it had drawn others, and Kamenwati had not been able to stop the vampire from destroying her family. She had been through so much already, and now she had to suffer this.

"Kam?"

Kamenwati usually cringed at the shortening of his name, but her quiet voice was a welcome relief from the screams that tore from her throat, and her mind. "Is this what dying is like?"

"You are not dying little one. I refuse to allow it." His voice was stern, aristocratic, the voice of a man who demanded obedience, but Alicia could hear the fear he was trying desperately to hide.

She reached out to pat his arm but a wave of pain chose that moment to rip through her, and instead of patting his arm she dug her claws in until the blood began to bubble around her fingernails. Lightning flashed in her eyes, the fire burning away his image until she was blind to anything but the flames inside.

" Alicia." His voice came from far away, floating, edged with panic.

Flames licked at her mind trying to burn away the memories of her life, trying to burn away her humanity.

"NO." She was not going to allow them to take anymore from her. She was not afraid to die, but she would not simply disappear into oblivion.

You cannot stop this, child. Soon you will be one of us.

Revulsion made her want to vomit as the voice of the *Seeker* crawled through her mind. *I will never become one of you,* she screamed back. *I will die first.*

Evil laughter danced in her mind, and the image of a hateful smirk floated in front of her. *Oh you* will *die, child. And when you do I shall claim your power.*

Someone moved towards her in the flames. Alicia squinted trying to focus on the image.

Was that Mama walking toward her? It was so hard to see her face. The flames were making it fuzzy. Alicia began to panic when she realized she was having a hard time remembering what her Mama looked like.

Mama. "Don't leave me," she whispered frantically.

Kamenwati's voice sounded as if it were encased in cotton. A fragile lifeline in a vast ocean of fear that she clung to with both hands. *It's going to be all right, little one. I will never leave you.* His words were comforting, and she let herself drift through her memories, no longer alone.

Kamenwati ignored the claws drawing blood from his arm, and struggled to keep his mind linked with Alicia's in a feeble attempt to dampen her pain. Although she seemed unaware of his presence he was sure that on some level she was aware of his presence. He wanted to share this battle to keep her memories alive, to keep the part of her that was human alive.

She was two. She was running across the front yard, chasing a butterfly as it flitted through the air, landing just out of reach before flitting off again when she got too close. Alicia laughed, and ran after it on short stubby legs. She heard a low growl and stopped. Terror wrapped its icy fingers around her tiny little heart, and squeezed until she didn't think she would ever be able to breathe again. She did not see the dog. All she saw were its huge white fangs, and the saliva dripping from the monster's jowls.

She turned, her short legs pumping as quickly as possible, but she knew she would not escape the beast. She was too slow. It was too fast. She could feel its hot breath on the back of her neck. Fear made her stumble. Instinct made her turn. The beast leaped at her throat and Alicia instinctively threw her hands up to protect herself. Her eyes widened in shocked disbelief when the dog stopped in midair, and then flew backwards to land on the ground several feet away.

She was shivering with fear. Papa ran and snatched her into his arms. He lifted her high above the ground away from where the vicious dog lay snarling. She could hear voices around her, the screams, and the accusations. She didn't know how her papa had stopped the dog chasing her, but she was glad he had.

It was you, little one. See the truth.

What did Kamenwati mean it was her? Papa had saved her. She couldn't save herself. She was too little.

Alicia drifted through her memories of Papa, forcing herself to remember when his face began to blur with wave after wave of pain that tore through her, leaving her weak and confused.

The sound of her mother's screams woke Alicia from a deep sleep. She sat up in bed, and clutched the blankets to her, afraid to move. *What is happening? Why are there flames outside my bedroom window? Why are the neighbors yelling?*

Mama and Papa ran into her room. Mama pulled the blanket from her numb fingers, and lifted her nightgown over her head. "Hurry," Papa whispered in a voice laced with fear. Alicia could hear her Papa dragging the drawers open. She tried to see what he was doing, but Mama chose that moment to drop the sundress over her head. Alicia automatically lifted her arms to help dress herself and Mama lifted her into her arms. While she watched in shocked silence Papa tossed a sack out her window, and climbed out. *Why didn't he use the door*, she wondered. The moment Papa's feet touched the ground he lifted his arms toward the window and Mama dropped her down to Papa. He set her on the ground beside the pack while he helped Mama out the window. Alicia stared, mesmerized by the flames that devoured her bedroom.

You caused this child. Alicia shuddered at the dark words spoken in that evil voice.

Alicia clutched her lifeline as the flames lick over, and through her body. *Did I do it? Did I bring this on my family?* Once the doubts began they grew rapidly. If she was the one who stopped the dog, then she was the one who brought the angry mob to their home, just like she was the one who brought that *monster* to their door when she was eight. She was evil. She deserved to die. Mama and Papa would be alive if it were not for her.

Yes. The velvety voice oozed, driving despair deeper into her soul. *You are Evil. Embrace your destiny, child. Come to me now.*

"No." Kamenwati would not allow her to go to *him.* He placed a hand on each side of Alicia's face, a face so hot it would have seared the skin off a human, and forced her to look at him. "Listen to me, Alicia. You are not evil. You did not do this." She moaned, and her eyes closed. " Look at me," he snapped. "Open your eyes, and see me. See yourself through my eyes."

Alicia's eyelids fluttered, but stayed closed. She wanted to open her eyes, but she was afraid of what would happen. The flames were too bright. If she opened her eyes they would burn out her pupils, and she would be blind. Or worse, they would escape and burn Kamenwati, and she would be alone again. *I can't,* she moaned.

You can.
Come to me.
Stay with me.
Evil.
Not evil.
The voices warred inside her head making her head ache, and Alicia wanted to scream at them to stop. She let go of her lifeline, and sank beneath the waves of flame. As her head

disappeared beneath the flames she thought she heard Kamenwati's voice demanding that she fight, but it was far away, and hard to hear over the evil, sinister laughter that had chased her relentlessly her entire life. She was so tired of it all. Maybe she could just take a little rest.

Beneath the sea of flames she risked a peak, and was surprised at how calm and clear everything was. Mama's face, Papa's voice, they were perfect.

~~

Conall stood in the darkened alley, and cursed. *Where in hell did she go?* He knew a female had been in this alley recently. Her scent was strong in both the alley, and on the human cleaning coconuts off the dock. Cloaking himself in a chimera mist, he moved closer to the human male. There were fresh bite marks on his neck. That they were easily visible to anyone who looked was not good, but the fact he was still alive was promising.

Conall took a peak into the man's memories and caught a glimpse of a cat. The man believed a stray cat bit him in the alley. It would have been comical if it the implications were not so serious.

She should not be able to weave memories like these so soon after her transition, if indeed she had survived the transition intact. This meant someone was either with her, or following her. That someone had to be very powerful to be able to disguise their presence, and that worried Conall.

A lot.

Sixteen

Kamenwati felt Alicia let go, and icy fingers clutched his heart making it difficult to breath, and nearly impossible to focus. What was wrong with him? He had never felt like this before. He was a God. He was one of the most powerful beings in the universe. He was not afraid of anything.

Until now. He watched Alicia's head dip beneath a sea of flames that existed only in her mind, and he was terrified. He just found her. He refused to lose her now.

Her auburn hair spread out on the surface fanning the flames in the growing inferno. Kamenwati mentally reached out and grabbed it, yanking her head above the surface, ignoring her spluttering.

Alicia's head broke through the surface of flames, and she gasped as the fire burned her throat and lungs. She shoved at the hand tangled in her hair. *Let go.* She shoved the command with the full force of her mind, the flames making it impossible to speak without inhaling them. Anger quickly replaced the fear that coursed through her veins. *Are you trying to drown me?* She spat.

Right. As if she could drown in a sea of flames. She was more likely to become a shish-ka-bob, or a lump of charcoal. Her fury grew until her vision blurred. What was wrong with her? All she had to do was extinguish the flames. She could do it. How hard could it be? She could do things that other's could not do. She could talk to people with her mind, move small objects, and see the past. Putting out a fire should be a piece of cake.

Alicia let the flames roll over her, in her, through her. She felt herself rising above the surface of the fiery sea. She sucked the flames inside of her until her lungs were full, and then she pushed—hard. Flames shot from her eyes, her fingertips, the very ends of her hair, from every pore of her body.

Kamenwati barely had time to throw up a shield to keep the flames from devouring him. This had never happened before. The flames were not real. They were a product of Alicia's mind. They were a part of the transition from human to Mage, a way of cleansing her soul. But Alicia's mind made the fire real and dangerous. Kamenwati had never witnessed such power in a newly born Mage before, and he was truly impressed. No wonder the *Seeker* as she referred to the Betrayer had been stalking her for so long. Even as a child her power had been great. That untapped potential had been a beacon for every power-crazed creature on earth. It was about time she used it to her own advantage.

Kamenwati watched helplessly, unable to use his own powers while hers were so out of control, afraid that he would cause more damage than good. Alicia's body continued to hover above the bed, firing pouring from every pore of her skin, igniting the bed, the walls, and even the ceiling.

Alicia kept the flames streaming through her for several moments before finally collapsing on the mattress. Now that her own power had diminished, Kamenwati doused the flames with a mere thought, and wiped all traces of fire from the room. A moment later, a bowl of clear water and a clean cloth appeared beside him. He could have cleaned her body with only a thought, but he preferred to do this job himself. Gently, almost reverently, he washed the soot from her still glowing skin; skin that was warm to touch, but no longer feverish. He hoped the worst was over. With gentle fingers, he brushed the hair from her temple, and her eyelids fluttered, and then opened. The hunger he saw in those dark orbs called forth an answering hunger that made his groin ache, and his fangs lengthen.

Alicia wet her lips with the tip of her tongue. A wave of lust rolled over Kamenwati, and filled the air with hot spices. She could hardly believe how incredibly sexy the man was. He was absolutely drop-dead gorgeous, and he was in her bedroom nearly naked. In her mind that made him fair game.

Her eyes roved over his granite features, stopping when they came to the small cuts where her fingernails had dug into his arms. Hunger and lust beat against her, tightening her womb, and lengthening her own fangs. Every breath she took filled her with the scent of blood, musk, and mouth watering spices until she was quivering with hunger and need. Alicia leaned in and nuzzled his chest letting his scent wash over her. Her fangs exploded, their tips piercing her lower lip. Alicia gasped at the pain, and then licked the tiny droplets of blood from her lip. She nearly had an orgasm just from the taste. It was like nothing she had ever tasted, and she wanted more.

Alicia slid her leg over Kamenwati's rubbing herself against his heated skin. With a little nudge she flipped him onto his back, and straddled his enormous erection, but not quite touching the tip. She leaned over him, inhaling his unique aroma, filling her lungs. Her fangs ached, and grew longer, until they were scraping against the skin stretched taut over the muscles on Kamenwati's chest. Her womb clenched, and she trembled helplessly as his hands came up and his hot palms trailed over her hips. Alicia snuck a peek from beneath her heavy lashes, and a different fire raced in her veins as his golden orbs flared with desire. Her own pupils widened in response, and fire pooled at her center. She melted beneath that look.

His skin looked as hard and cold as marble, but the heat radiating from him was enough to sear human skin. Her fingers splayed across his chest to rest on either side of his sun tattoo, and she listened to the erratic beat of his heart. Alicia traced the outline of that fiery tattoo, and then trailed her fingers along his ribcage, and lower, slipping her hand beneath his loincloth she gently cupped his balls in the palm of her hand.

Kamenwati's golden orbs flared brighter, and he groaned. She could feel the heat from his tip against her core, and she bit down on her lip to keep from groaning aloud.

It was the wrong thing to do.

Blood, even her blood, was an aphrodisiac sending lust coursing through her. The flames of desire spread until she was sure they would devour her, and this time she wouldn't be able to stop them.

Not a bad way to die.

I will not hurt you, little one.

Alicia knew Kamenwati would not hurt her. He would never get the chance. She was going to spontaneously combust, and it would be over. Already the fire in her core was growing stronger. *God he smelled delicious.* Alicia nuzzled his neck.

Just one little sip, that's all I need. Just a tiny drop to keep me going. Alicia let her teeth scrape the throbbing vein in Kamenwati's neck.

This is what Kamenwati was waiting for. *Drink, little one,* his velvet smooth voice sent quivers racing through her body, cooling the flames only to have them flare up again. *I offer myself so you may live.*

Alicia's lips parted, closing over that throbbing vein. She felt his skin pushing against her fangs. She could already taste the rich coppery liquid that lived there; the power that coursed through those veins.

That's right. Drink. Drink it all. The dark sinister voice of her nightmares ran through her mind, urging her on, encouraging the hunger that clawed at her belly.

Just one little sip. I can stop after one little sip.

Alicia sank her teeth into pure heaven. Light exploded behind her eyes. Power surged through her with each swallow. Kamenwati groaned from pain or ecstasy, Alicia couldn't be sure.

Drain him. The dark voice urged gleefully.

Shock halted her actions. *No! I am not a monster.*

There was a flash of light, and Alicia disappeared.

Seventeen

A flash of lightning over the horizon wouldn't normally be a cause for concern, but tonight was different. There was power running rampant through the night air, uncontrolled, unleashed, and that was dangerous for them all. Not to mention the tight feeling he had in his gut. The one that told him the Betrayer was near. But how was that even possible? The Betrayer had locked in the Shadows between the Earth and the Chimera for centuries. His presence should not be so strong here on earth. Not unless something, or someone, was acting as a conduit for him. Was this then, why his prince had sent him to earth so near to the coming nightfall?

Conall's eyes flickered to the night sky, and his heart nearly stopped. Not something that happened to him often. He didn't have much time. He had less than twenty-four earth hours to find Alaric's daughter, and drag her home.

That's if she survived the transition, did not turn vampire, and wanted to meet her father. At least he knew he was looking for a female, which made him wonder why Alaric had not sent for her sooner. Female magi were coveted for their very uniqueness. Not many of them survived the transition at all.

The time limit posed another problem. Travel. He was going to have to travel as a human. Once he stepped into the Gloaming, those doorways through time and space the Magi preferred to travel, time would stand still while it kept on moving here on earth. Not a problem if he knew exactly where he was going. He could be there in a heartbeat. On the other hand, searching could take several earth days—days he did not have. He needed to find Alaric's daughter, and get back into the Chimera before nightfall. His place was beside his Prince in the coming battle, not gallivanting around earth looking for someone who might not want to be found.

Conall manipulated the energy around him, and a Honda two stroke appeared in front of him, black of course, with a matching black helmet. *Where are you girl?* He started the bike, appreciating the way it purred quietly, and the vibration between his strong legs. His black duster twisted and warped forming itself into a black motorcycle jacket that wouldn't interfere with his ride. Conall twisted the right handle and revved the engine. Satisfied with the way it sounded he donned the helmet, and took off in a cloud of dust.

Using the fingerprint of magic he felt in the alley as a beacon he left the small fishing village behind, and aimed his bike toward the mountains. Conall liked it here, the quiet of the night, and the warmth of the breeze against his cheeks. By morning it would be hot as hell but that didn't concern Conall. As a Mage he could control his environment if the need arose, but he wouldn't waste the energy it took to do so. He liked the feel of the wind on his face, and come morning if he was still here he would savor the feel of the hot sun. The Chimera was beautiful, but there were no such changes. The sun shone without ever getting too hot. The rain fell when needed without feeling warm or cool against your skin. The Chimera went through the seasons without any real change at all and Conall treasured his times on Earth, if only for its inconsistent weather.

~~~

The wheels of the Cessna rolled to a stop and Jade stood up, or rather tried to. Luke unsnapped his seatbelt, and quickly reached over to unsnap his wife's. He was worried about Jade. She had been an automaton since bursting from the clearing to tell them she was going to Mexico. When he called Daniel on his cell, he was already preparing the Cessna for takeoff having received his orders directly from Jade.

They would fly to Mexico to drop Jade off, and then Daniel was to fly the rest of them home.

Yeah right. Like he had any intention of leaving his mate alone in Mexico. Daniel could take the children back, but he was staying with Jade. Luke looked up to see three pairs of eyes glaring at him. *Maybe sending them home wasn't going to be all that easy.*

The moment Jade's seatbelt was free she stood up, and strode toward the door of the plane. Her body was here functioning on some level, but her mind was on the back of a motorbike flying along a dirt road somewhere in Mexico. The glimpses Luke was getting from Jade's mind were confusing and disorienting. They were rushing past trees and hills, and small lonely farms heading toward something.

Crap. Was this how it was when they summoned Jade? This confusing chaos of the mind, being in two places at once. How did she function at all?

When the door slid silently open Jade breathed in the cool Mexican air. Dawn was a mere glimmer over the horizon, and already she could taste the heat it would bring. Jade turned to Luke who was crowding her at the door, followed closely by all three of their children. She placed her hands on the scratchy surface of his cheeks, and rubbed her palms on the stubble.

Had it only been two days since Luke shaved, and they traced Alicia to Romania? God she was tired. Maybe she should take something before she got on a plane. Something that would help her sleep. Not that she would have taken anything this trip. She could not afford to lose her connection with the man on the dirt bike. He was her only lead.

Jade stood on her tiptoes, and tugged Luke's face lower until their lips met. *I love you.*

Luke closed his eyes and tasted the sweetness of his wife's lips, and tried to shut out what was coming next.

Take care of the children.

Always. Luke had every intention of taking care of his young. They would be safe with Daniel.

Daniel. Luke narrowed his eyes, and watched his wife. He could feel the power flowing from her. *Take this plane out of here.*

Yes Boss. Boss?

Daniel?

Bring Alicia home, and stay safe. Althea would never forgive me if anything happened to you.

I will.

Jade's amber eyes were swirling with power; power that made the inside of the plane shimmer. "I love you," she said. "Now go home." Jade shifted as she stepped through the doorway, and flew away.

Luke jumped back when the door slid shut. "What in hell?" He tried to open the door but it wouldn't budge.

Damn you, Jade. Open this door.

Jade's voice was a mere whisper inside his head, as if she were preoccupied, or couldn't afford the energy a conversation with him took while flying. *Go home, Lykos. Keep our children safe.*

My god. She hasn't' eaten. Jade never ate while on a plane, and her body needed fuel—lot's of fuel. Luke growled, and smashed his fist against the door. It didn't budge. *Eat.* He ordered her. *That is an order, Jade. You get something to eat. Now!*

Jade's laughter echoed in the corners of his mind, but it did nothing to soothe his temper. *I so love a man who thinks he can order me around.*

Daniel came out of the cockpit. "It's no use Boss man. This isn't the first time she has done this. That seal will not break until we leave."

Luke growled at Daniel who just shrugged. Luke's eyes flashed. "Then take this bird up. Now."

Daniel was from the Lycan Pack in Willow Bend. At one time Luke was his Alpha. But that was before Daniel left the pack to become a member of the O'Connor Search and Rescue team. A move Luke sanctioned at the time, not yet realizing he too would leave the pack to be with Jade. A move he did not regret, although sometimes he could throttle that female.

Luke moved toward his seat, the triplets were already buckled in.

"How far does this bird need to get before the seal is broken?" Gheorgès asked. " Once around the airport?"

It actually took five.

Eighteen

Alicia crouched on the cool black marble floor, her hair dancing wildly around her head, her dark eyes blazing, her fangs elongated and dripping red. She was totally focused on the male dressed all in white standing before her with his arm raised as if to throw a weapon. The splendor of the room meant nothing to her as she glared straight ahead trying to figure out how she got here. The last thing she remembered was the *Seeker* urging her to drain the life from Kamenwati and thinking, *God, if I were with my father right now I would kill him.* Guess she had better be careful what she wished for, or even thought for that matter.

The raised hand before her was empty but that didn't mean anything. The air in the room crackled with power, and tiny lightning sparks bounced off the walls; whether from him or her Alicia wasn't sure. A door burst open with surprising speed considering how monstrous it was, and a lanky red head rushed in with a gun in each hand.

Get out!

The male flew backward out the door, his white fangs flashing in his astonished face. The massive doors slammed shut. *Wow. Did I do that?* Alicia didn't have time to worry about what just happened. She tracked the male with her eyes and senses as he slowly lowered his hand to a less threatening position.

So this was her father; the monster whose blood ran in her veins. Funny, he didn't look like a monster. He had the face of an angel—a dark angel. Then again, so had the monster that killed her beloved Mama and Papa; the face of an angel, and the dark soul of a demon. It was easy to see how her mother fell for his lies when he came to her wearing that face.

Alicia was not going to be that stupid. She would never believe anything that came out of that mouth. Her gaze narrowed to the tips of his fangs, and her blood began a slow boil. He sank those fangs into her mother's smooth throat, and drank her essence.

Like I drank Kamenwati's, came the unbidden thought. *Oh my God. I am a monster just like my father.* She looked around the room, frantically searching for an escape route. "I hate you," she spat just before she vanished.

The massive door to the throne room burst open so suddenly that Tex and two other Magi nearly landed face down on the black marble floor. Tex's eyes tracked the large chamber but the Prince was alone. The only evidence that the nearly naked female was real was the remnants of power still sparking throughout the chamber.

Alaric was staring at the empty spot where his daughter had stood, crouched actually. She never did get out of her defensive position, and for a heartbeat he had thought she was going to actually attack him.

His daughter. *My God she was beautiful, like his sweet Maria. The power emanating from her was mind boggling.* He wasn't sure that if it came down to a battle between them that she would not beat him; at least once she learned to control it. He did know that if she was crazed he would not be the one to bring her down.

He wouldn't be able to do it.

His daughter.

She hadn't looked crazed. She was definitely pissed, and just before she vanished he thought she looked horrified.

But not crazed.

Who had she fed from? Not Conall. Conall was a very powerful Mage, and his best friend, but Alaric did not detect any of Conall in her.

" Where did she go?" Tex asked, still tracking the four corners of the large chamber for signs of movement in the shadows.

Alaric shrugged. *Where did she go?* "The better question is `how did she get in here?'"

" Could she have got hold of a crystal?" Ramka asked while rubbing his forehead as was his habit when thinking.

"No crystal was used." Alaric was distracted, and didn't notice the look of bafflement on the Magi's faces. His daughter had not used the crystal, although he had glimpsed it nestled in the hollow of her throat. He was remembering the day he gave the crystal to his sweet Maria.

" Give this to our daughter on her twenty-first birthday. Tell her to put it on and say my name, Alaric." Granted he did not always keep track of the passage of time on earth but he had a reason to watch now, and she should have called to him at least three cycles ago. When she did not he had accepted the fact that his daughter had not survived. Then the crystal woke, and he sent Conall to find her.

She should have called to him. *Why hadn't she called to him?*

His daughter should have put on the crystal, and said his name, and he would have gone to her. Under no circumstances should she have been able to come to him, to throw his man out, and slam those massive doors. Alaric's chest filled with pride for the child he had sired. *You are magnificent.*

To the Magi he said, " Get the candles."

If the three of them were confused before, the look of astonishment on their faces showed they had not realized how serious the situation was. Alaric could not remember the last time he had summoned Ra.

Less than a chime later seven Magi in white robes stood in a circle of stone, seven golden candles flickered in the absolute blackness of the underground chamber. Their melodic chanting had barely begun began when there was a flash brighter than an exploding sun, and a male figure appeared.

The Magi bowed before their God.

"My Lord," Alaric's tone was unassuming as was expected in the presence of a God.

Ra had no such inclination. " Cut the crap, Alaric." His deep voice reverberated in the chamber. "Why have you summoned me? You should be preparing for the coming battle."

Alaric cleared his throat, but his voice still cracked. Ra would kill him for allowing this breach to happen. It was his fault the seal was broken. He was the one who had left a crystal on earth. "The seal, My Lord, it's been broken."

Ra's lips turned up slightly in the corners. "Tell me something I don't already know." Ra seemed to notice the presence of the Magi priests in their white robes for the first time. "Leave us," he barked the command and the room emptied, all but Alaric.

Wasn't this a day for surprises the priests thought as they found themselves outside the chamber doors.

"Is there something you wish to say to me?" Ra's voice was an echo in the silent chamber.

Alaric thought of those flashing eyes in the perfection of that alabaster skin. "Forgive me, My Lord." Ra cocked his head, and lifted one eyebrow waiting, and Alaric continued. "It is my fault the seal has been broken. I left a crystal on earth a quarter century ago."

Ra's laughter rolled like thunder until the walls themselves shook. "Hardly. If it is anyone's fault it is mine. When I created the seal centuries ago I was so full of myself I did not even consider the possibility of it weakening. Regardless, it was not the crystal that allowed the seal to be broken."

Alaric bowed his head until his eyes were in line with his toes. "I went to Earth." Alaric paused. Ra said nothing to interrupt as his friend continued. "I found an angel there ... Maria. When I left she was with child. A girl. I could taste her in her mother's blood. I couldn't stand the thought of losing her. I left behind a key to the portal in the form of a small crystal pendant. When it didn't wake I believed my daughter was dead." Alaric raised his eyes to his God, and braced his back. "I just saw her. She was in the throne room. She sent my guards flying through the doors, and locked them out, all without raising a finger." Alaric's voice rang with pride.

Ra nodded his head. "Indeed you have a lot to be proud my old friend."

Alaric shrugged. "Wouldn't you be proud if Kamenwati surpassed all your expectations?"

"Indeed I am, as you have a right to be." Ra held his palm flat and an image played in the air above it, like a three dimensional movie showing Alicia before her transformation facing the wrath of Ra with no fear whatsoever. "She is a true warrior. That may be the only thing that saves her."

Nineteen

Oh God. This is incredible. Never before had anyone drank from Kamenwati's vein. It was the most erotic feeling, her hot breath on his neck, the gentle tug at his throat as she drew his rich blood into herself. The initial sharp stab as her fangs pierced his skin quickly turned to streams of pleasure. Wave after wave of unimaginable pleasure coursed through his body. If he was any harder he would explode.

Kamenwati rolled his hips aiming himself for her core, wanting all of him in her; his flesh as well as his blood. He willed away his loin cloth. Alicia stiffened. There was a flash of light.

Alicia vanished.

Kamenwati lay on the small bed staring at the cracks in the ceiling. *No!* His mind screamed, lightning flashed, and thunder rumbled, even while he tried to figure out what in hell had happened.

The rumbling grew louder until it was a roar. Kamenwati forced his mind still while he felt the air around the small farmhouse. Someone was coming.

Black fighting leathers, motor cycle boots, and a long black leather duster materialized on his lean body. Kamenwati checked his weapons although he knew exactly what he had summoned; a knife, a sword, and his weapon of choice—a morning star. A morning star was a spiked metal ball on a length of thick chain. The chain wrapped itself around his thick forearm, and he gently swung the ball back and forth checking its weight.

Severing the head was the quickest way to ensure the death of their enemies. A bullet through the head and heart almost simultaneously would put them down, but incineration was the only way to ensure they didn't rise again. Death was such a fickle thing. Beheading worked. Once the head left the body both would spontaneously combust, becoming nothing more than ash, but first you had to bring them down.

Kamenwati strode through the door in full fighting mode just as a black figure on an even blacker motorbike turned into the yard from the dirt road that ran past the farm.

The motorbike skidded to a halt, and the driver casually reached up and removed his helmet shaking out his long black hair. He eyed Kamenwati's clothing and weapons. "You expecting someone else?"

Kamenwati swung the morning star with deliberate menace. "You call that a motor cycle?"

"Hey, don't be dissin' my ride, Kam. She may not be pretty but she's great on the hills."

Kamenwati cringed at the shortening of his name. Only two people in the universe dared call him Kam. Sounded like a car part when Conall said it, but he rather liked the way it came out when Alicia said it. When she said it in that soft whispery voice of hers it was an intimate caress.

Conall threw his leg off his ride at the same time Kamenwati stepped forward. Hey met like warriors with their hands clasping forearms, and then they embraced, slapping each other on the back.

" Con you old bastard how you been? Still chasing after the skirts?"

Conall had survived his change more than two centuries before, and was brought into the *Chimera* by his father, but not before he had gotten a reputation for loving and leaving. When the townsfolk saw him coming, the mothers locked up their daughters while the fathers headed for their guns. After the change the need for blood accompanied his growing sexual appetite, making him more of a menace.

Conall was a rogue when it came to women, but he had a code of honor that he lived by even after the change came. He never went after the truly innocent or married women, and he never allowed himself to drink enough to weaken them. The blood enhanced the sex, but it did nothing to sustain him and by the time his father found him he was dying, still determined not to take a life in order to save his own. Refusing to listen to the compelling voices in his head and turn vampire.

Kamenwati had fought by Conall's side during the long years of battle against Ra's betrayer, and they fast became friends. Conall fought with the same single minded determination he did everything else, and he soon drew the attention of the Prince of the Magi, Alaric. When Alaric realized Conall's potential he immediately brought him to the palace as part of his personal guard. Alaric like everyone else that met Conall, was drawn to his boyish charm, and his enthusiasm for everything he did, and they began a friendship that continued to this day.

It didn't take long for Alaric to realize Conall was not cut out for the mundane life the palace offered. It wasn't uncommon for the Magi to spend time on earth. There were not many females in the *Chimera*, and the Magi were males with the same needs as all males. Conall was the perfect Mage to send to earth to seek out the offspring of the Magi and help them embrace their new lives. He was unattached, loyal, and he craved women.

Kamenwati's eyes narrowed. " Who brings you here?" He already knew. No coincidence would bring Conall to this remote part of the world at this exact time.

" Alaric's daughter."

A blast of heat so powerful Conall staggered beneath it radiated from Kamenwati's chest, and Conall laughed. "Oh shit," he sputtered. "This day just keeps on getting better." Kamenwati glared. Conall shrugged and continued. "First Alaric finally owns up to being as much of a male as the rest of us, and admits he has a daughter, and then you go and fall for her."

As realization dawned Conall quit sputtering. "Crap. She's the one isn't she? The one you've been watching over all this time."

Kamenwati knew the instant Alicia returned. He felt her materialize beside him, and saw her crouched ready to attack Conall. Her hair stood on end as power crackled in the air around her, and her fangs were elongated. Her naked body radiated with the power of the sun.

A low whistle escaped Conall's pursed lips. *My God she's magnificent. I can see why everyone wants her.*

Alicia caught Conall's passing thought, and she stole a glance at Kamenwati. He was staring at her with such heat in his eyes, and he didn't appear in the least concerned with the stranger's presence. Alicia took her cue from Kamenwati, and forced herself to relax. Her hair settled into its usual curly mass, and the air around her began to calm. She realized she was naked, and wished she had her clothes. There was a gentle shift in the air as a pair of pale blue jeans, and a long white button-up shirt settled over her skin.

Well done, little one. Kamenwati's deep voice caressed her, and she could feel his warm fingers on the back of her neck. She snuck a peek from beneath her long lashes while keeping an eye on the stranger. Kamenwati had not moved, but she could still feel that gentle pressure on her neck. *Where have you been?*

I've been to London to visit the King. Kamenwati's deep laughter reverberated through her body making her *hot*. She swallowed. The man didn't even have to touch her and he could make her tremble with need.

The stranger cleared his throat, and both sets of eyes flipped to him. *Damn. How could I forget we are not alone?* "Who are you?" Alicia demanded.

"Conall. I am ..."

"He's a friend of mine," Kamenwati interjected before Conall could spill that Alaric sent him. Instinct alone warned him Alicia wasn't going to be very welcoming of anyone sent by her father.

"So my *father* sent you." She spat the word father with such venom even Kamenwati cringed. *No sense trying to hide shit from me Kam. Seems I can see what's on your mind.*

Don't worry. I promise not to disintegrate him because he knows the monster that fathered me.

There was an audible hum in the air, and Conall found himself suddenly looking for a place to escape. Funny, he never felt like a third wheel around any of the mated males in the *Chimera*, and yet he definitely felt like an extra spoke here. The sun's fingers crept over the horizon, and Conall cleared his throat. "Time is running Kamenwati."

"Well I am not." Alicia watched the trail of the already hot sun crawl across the land turning the dried brown grasses a deep rich golden as they stirred in its first rays. Her eyes were watering and she wiped the liquid away with the back of her hand. A grackle whistled from somewhere nearby, a rooster crowed hello to the morning, and the chickens stirred from their resting places to begin scratching at the dirt in search of substance. Everywhere she looked life went on, and it was about time she took a stand, and took her own life back.

"Maam," Conall spoke with quiet urgency, as if he knew she would argue if he tried to tell her what to do. Besides, with the possessive way Kamenwati was standing, so close to her side he was practically a part of her, he knew he wouldn't get anywhere.

"You can leave." Alicia's dark eyes flashed with barely controlled power, and her right hand was rubbing small circles over her stomach like she had eaten something that didn't agree with her.

Kamenwati stepped even closer, his eyes anxious. He felt the glitch in the universe. The betrayer was near, but something else was coming; something powerful. "What do you feel?"

Dark eyes swirling with power and emotion pegged him. "Something is coming ... evil ... the *Seeker* ... many others ... we don't have much time." Alicia gave her head a small shake like she was clearing cobwebs and her swirling eyes settled back to their normal dark coffee. "We don't have much time." She turned her attention to the tall man dressed all in black, with long black hair that hung past his shoulders, only he wasn't a man. He was like her, a victim of his father's lust. " Conall. Emissary of Alaric, Prince of the Magi." She had picked the knowledge from his mind. Conall betrayed his surprise with a mere flicker of his dark eyes, but he did not interrupt. "I know who you are. I read it in your mind. I make no apology. You are a stranger, and you have sought me out. I have a right to know who is enemy, and who is not."

"And I am?"

Alicia kept her eyes locked with Conall's. "You don't want to be my enemy, but you will if the need arises. You are Kamenwati's friend. You are loyal, and you would give your life for what you believe is right." Her stomach was a pot of boiling acid, the bile beginning to rise in her throat until she thought it would spew out of her mouth. " Stay or go. It is no concern of mine. I already know Kamenwati will not leave, but I refuse to run anymore."

The presence was so strong Conall wouldn't be surprised if something suddenly reached out and touched him. " Something's coming." He knew it as well as he knew his own name, he just didn't know what. He could feel the Betrayer, the *Seeker* as Alicia referred to him. An apt name he thought, as the Betrayer sought out newly matured Magi and tried to convert them to vampirism, or just have them killed so he could take their power when it released back into the universe. He knew the fingerprint of the *Seeker's* power, but this other was unknown to him.

There was a brief flicker of surprised recognition, and then relief in Alicia's dark eyes. If Conall had not been looking at her at that moment he would have missed it, but it was there. She recognized the power signature. Of course Kamenwati would have sensed it. It was even conceivable that Kamenwati would know what was coming, but that didn't necessarily mean he would tell them.

The vibration in the air was so tiny a human would not have noticed the difference in the atmosphere. He was Mage. He noticed, and frowned.

Kamenwati's body shifted into a fighting stance, and Alicia reached over and placed her small hand on the soft leather of his duster. Kamenwati relaxed, slightly. "We have about two hours."

Alicia's voice was soft, and the eyes she turned on Kamenwati were a blatant invitation. His blood thickened in his veins, and his cock thickened beneath the leathers. His morning star vanished, and ignoring the smirk on Conall's face he scooped Alicia in his strong arms, and strode toward the small farmhouse. "You can bunk in the barn," he said over his shoulder.

Twenty

Kamenwati gently lowered Alicia onto the small bed, and dropped his duster and the rest of his weapons to the floor. He couldn't wait to crush up against Alicia on that small bed, skin to skin, mouth to mouth. He wanted inside her with a vengeance, still needy from their earlier encounter. He needed his blood inside her, his body inside hers. He had glimpsed what it would be like when she drank from him earlier, and he was so ready to finish what they had started.

Kamenwati tugged his shirt over his head, and froze, staring at Alicia. *You are beautiful.* His voice was a husky whisper. He loved the heat that crawled up her neck and infused her cheeks with color. Her fingers were busy working on the buttons of her shirt.

"No," Kamenwati growled low in his throat. He knelt over her, captured both her hands in one of his much larger ones, and stretched her arms above her head, lifting her breasts and pulling her shirt tight across those taut nipples. "Let me."

With exquisite slowness he unbuttoned her shirt with his free hand, while his lips and tongue discovered every inch of her silken skin as it was slowly revealed.

Alicia gasped when his rough tongue flicked over her taut nipple. Kamenwati called in the *Chimera* to blanket the small house from prying eyes and ears, ever conscious of Conall moving around in the barn.

Kamenwati flicked the taut pink nipple a couple more times before changing the rhythm to long slow licks like he was savoring an ice cream cone, swirling his tongue around the tip, and then sucking in while Alicia moaned and squirmed beneath him. His own body pounded with the urgent need to claim her, and he pulled the rest of her shirt open ignoring the buttons that popped off, and rolled on the floor.

Kamenwati kept his mouth on her breast suckling like a newborn while one hand slid down her taut stomach to slip beneath the waistband of her jeans, and stroke her sex, quickly bringing her to a lust filled stupor. Alicia couldn't get enough. She had a voracious appetite for sex—and blood. As the inferno in her grew so did her fangs. It didn't help when Kamenwati's hot lips released her breast to follow the blistering trail left by his magic fingers.

Moaning and twisting she tried to get closer. She wanted his lips where his fingers were. She wanted them everywhere. The denim of her jeans was too constricting. No sooner had the thought crossed her mind and the problem was solved.

No jeans.

In a blink of an eye Kamenwati's lips were on her sex, his tongue flickering in and out tasting her spicy honey. Alicia's body jerked and shuddered as the inferno grew until she erupted like a volcano.

Kamenwati crawled up Alicia's quaking body licking his tongue along her heated skin, twirling it in her belly button, flicking the taut nipples, and finally capturing her moans as he caught her lips. His tongue traced the tips of her fangs, and he could taste her hunger, her need. His body grew harder at the thought of those fangs piercing his skin as he fed both her appetites at once.

With a simple thought his leathers went the way of his duster and weapons freeing his painful erection. Kamenwati was no saint but he had never wanted, never needed, a woman like he needed Alicia. She looked so fragile, so dainty, but her appearance hid an inner strength he found erotic. He was going to feed that strength, only this time he was going to be in her when he did it.

God was he hot. She was burning, consumed by flames, her bones were melting in their heat fusing the two of them together until she couldn't tell where she ended and he began. They were one body, one soul, one heartbeat forcing liquid strength through their veins. As their flesh pounded together, and their hearts beat louder Alicia's fangs exploded. That hot fiery liquid called to her, begged her to be taken, and Alicia didn't have the strength to deny her hunger.

Fangs pierced the vein running to Kamenwati's heart, and he exploded. As his life's essence flooded her mouth, his life giving seed filled her womb.

Twenty-One

On silent wings the white owl lit on a branch high in an apple tree that had long given up bearing fruit, where it should have a clear vision of the farmyard, the small stone farmhouse, and the larger barn. The feathers on the scruff of its neck ruffled.

Where was the farm?

There was a strange mist that gave the area a hazy, unreal look, and where the farm should be was fog. Bright yellow eyes concentrated on the mist in front of them and the farmyard appeared, and then the barn shimmered into view. If she relaxed the concentrated effort to see what was right in front of her, she would not even know it existed.

Chimera. Jade was familiar with the concept of blanketing yourself in illusion to appear invisible to the naked eye but it would take something very powerful to hide an entire house, let alone the barn and the yard.

The owl concentrated on the yard until it could see the chickens pecking in the dirt. It looked away, and back again, and the chickens were still there. The silence suddenly filled with the sounds of their clucking and scratching. The yellow eyes swirled as the owl concentrated on the house that continued to fade the moment her concentration left it. The power was emanating from there. She could sense it, but she could not identify its fingerprint.

All magical beings left a unique fingerprint, and each fingerprint was identifiable by species, and then in a more personal sense by individual. For example, the fingerprint left by a vampire was different than the fingerprint left by a Lycan, and each Lycan or vampire left their own individual fingerprint. It worked the same as fingerprints left by humans at crime scenes. Jade could not identify this particular signature.

One thing she was certain of, Alicia was in that house.

The owl tilted its head slightly focusing its stare where the barn should be. With an audible pop the mist burst, and the barn stood solid. The large doors flew open and the stranger she watched step through the breach in the universe strode into the yard. His leather coat was once again long and flowing, as was his black hair. He halted just outside the door, a sword in his right hand, and let his eyes track the yard. His aura shimmered with power, and Jade tossed up a little illusion of her own. She wasn't really surprised when his eyes passed the branch she was perched on, only to quickly return.

The owl's yellow stare locked with the dark stare of the stranger. The pull of those eyes was strong, mesmerizing. The owl tilted its head a little more to better focus, and its yellow eyes flared. The owl lifted from its perch as a fireball hit the branch it vacated.

Conall stepped back, another fireball at the ready when the owl shifted into a tall slender woman with strange amber eyes, and settled to the ground a couple feet in front of him. Her white blonde hair was streaked with gold and silver, and cropped very short.

"So you want to play ball." Her voice was soft, melodic, and he almost dropped the ball of fire he was readying.

Conall was fascinated with the way those amber eyes sparkled, and almost lost track of what her hands were doing. The top of his head felt the heat from a ball of fire that passed by way too close.

The two combatants circled each other warily, eyes locked together, as they sized each other up. Most of the battles Jade fought were on a physical level and she was a little rusty when it came to her magic, but that didn't mean she wasn't going to play the game. The sky above rumbled, and a streak of lightning struck the ground inches from Conall's feet. He jumped back, his eyes flashing with fury.

This was so not going to happen. He readied a blast, fully aware of the similar blast readied in the female's palm. It was like looking in a mirror. Eyes locked. Arms lifted. Palms opened.

The two fireballs hurtled toward each other like trains on a collision course.

Alicia felt the explosion of power as the fireball hit the apple tree. She tore her fangs from Kamenwati's vein, and looked up at him dizzy with power. "What was that? It sounded like a gas tank exploded."

Kamenwati was the first to pull his self together. Keeping between Alicia and the door he instantly donned his leathers, duster, and weapons. Another explosion rocked the small farmhouse, and lightning flashed outside the window. He turned to make sure Alicia was all right. She stood beside the bed dressed in jeans and a t-shirt, her dark hair a mass of uncontrolled curls, her cheeks slightly blushed. He wanted to kiss her, and drag her back to bed. He wanted to send her far away where she would be safe.

Neither one was an option. She had to fight her own battles; the best he could offer was to fight by her side.

Alicia's eyes widened with recognition, and she vanished. Kamenwati snarled. *I wish you would quit doing that.* He strode through the door and froze, his eyes taking in the scene before him. Conall was standing in front of the barn a *Moarte* across from him. Two fireballs were on a collision course between them, and Alicia materialized right in the middle of it all.

He couldn't move. He couldn't breathe. He couldn't just stand there and watch her die. He threw a shield around her just as the two fireballs sizzled and fell harmlessly to the ground.

Kamenwati wanted to blast both the *Moarte* and the Magi for putting Alicia in danger. What was the *Moarte* doing here anyway? Hers must be the power he felt earlier. A loud thumping drew his attention to Alicia trapped in a bubble of his making, and the thunderous look on her face made him wish he were brave enough to leave her in there for a while, at least until she cooled down. She did not look too pleased with his interference.

Kamenwati Horakhty you remove this barrier immediately or I will.

Shit. Alicia did not have enough control yet to pull off such a feat without consequences. Maybe it was time to show her what could happen if you could not control the magic.

The air inside the barrier started to glow as both Alicia's power and anger grew. The barrier began to vibrate as it tried to hold against her will. The air in the protective bubble was stagnant, and it was getting hard to breathe. Alicia gasped for air, and started to panic, losing the fragile hold on her magic. There was a blast of white light and the magic splintered, like shards of glass, pieces flying everywhere. Shards struck both the *Moarte* and the Magi, and they fell to the ground writhing in agony. Their magic haphazardly filling the atmosphere until chaos reigned. Chickens squawked in the yard, and ran for cover as feathers flew and the scent of cooked meat filled the air. Flames caught the dried grass quickly spreading across the yard to lick up the wooden boards of the barn until that too was an inferno, and then the flames headed toward the farmhouse.

It took less than ten seconds for the entire scene to play out in Alicia's mind. With a horrified gasp she quickly reigned in both her temper and her power, and waited meekly for Kamenwati to lower the barrier he had created.

The *Moarte* was staring at Alicia with all the protectiveness of a she-bear with her cub. So this is the one who saved Alicia from the vampire all those years ago, and she looked like she thought Alicia needed saving right now, from him and Conall.

The instant the shield dissolved the two females flew into each other's arms. They hugged, and the *Moarte* held Alicia back so she could check her for injury, and then they hugged again. There was both love and anxiety in her voice when the *Moarte* finally spoke. "If you ever pull a fool stunt like that again I'll ground you until you're eighty."

Kamenwati could get behind that. In the short time he'd been with Alicia she had managed to shear centuries off his life.

Alicia laughed, and finally released her hold on the *Moarte* conscious of the males watching them. She knew Jade was tracking them even though she wasn't looking at them. Jade would know exactly where they were, and what they were doing. "Grounded? Are you kidding me? I haven't been grounded since I was ten."

"Doesn't mean it can't be done young lady." The entire time she was lecturing Alicia, Jade was checking her for any damage she might have missed. "Seriously, Alicia," she scolded. "Whatever possessed you to jump into the middle of a firefight? What were you thinking?"

Alicia shrugged, and smirked at Conall. "I couldn't very well let you kill him now could I?"

Jade shook her head, and then turned her amber eyes on Conall. "He started it." She sounded like a recalcitrant child, and the pout on her lips had Alicia laughing. The unexpected sound of that laugh tugged at Kamenwati's heart strings. It was like a cool mist on a hot summer's night.

Alicia threw her hands up in the air like she had watched Jade do a thousand times when the triplets were fighting. "Fine," she mimicked. "Go at it then. See if I care." She stepped back, bowed at the waist, and swept her arm toward Conall. "Have at him, Mom. He's all yours."

"Mom," sputtered Conall his eyes wide.

"Mom," echoed Kamenwati at the same time. That he didn't know. He knew the *Moarte* had rescued Alicia when she was eight, but not once had Alicia let slip who her new family was, and Kamenwati would never have guessed the *Moarte* had adopted her.

Conall threw his own hands up in surrender. "If I apologize now can we call a truce and start over?"

Jade's amber eyes sparkled with mischief as she narrowed her gaze on him. "Hmm. Apologize for trying to knock me out of that tree, and I will consider it."

Whoa, Kamenwati shot at Conall. *You didn't. Tell me you did not attack a* Moarte. *What were you thinking?*

Apparently I wasn't, answered Conall in a droll voice. Conall had heard the stories of the *Moarte,* and was well aware of the power they possessed. Not only were they powerful and deadly, once they caught your scent there was no escaping their justice. It was hard to picture any of the *Moarte* he had heard about having a sense of humor. Lucky for him this one seemed to.

Jade shook her head sadly. *I wouldn't believe everything you hear Magi.*

Startled by her voice in his head, although he didn't know why he should be, Conall quickly recovered his equilibrium and bowed at the waist. "I offer my apologies for trying to knock you out of the tree," he said seriously, no hint of sarcasm or humor in his voice.

Jade's own lips twitched and then lifted into a crooked smile. " Glad you said tried. Apology accepted."

Jade. Are you all right? Answer me dammit. Luke sounded worried, and out of breath.

Jade's amber eyes took on a dreamy look. *I thought I sent you home husband. Where are you?*

We are still several miles away.

We? Jade's laughter tickled his mind. *I should have known. There's not one in the lot of you that ever listens.*

"Hey. I listen."

Jade raised her brows at her daughter. "And how many times have I told you that it is not polite to listen in on another's conversation?"

Alicia shrugged, and grimaced, and rubbed at her temples. " What can I say? You are so loud right now that a human couldn't shut you out."

The color drained from her face, and her eyes rolled back in her head. Kamenwati stepped closer and she staggered against him.

Luke. I need you to go get Matthew and bring him to the farmhouse. Tell him to bring the med kit. And be careful. Something big is coming. There was no sense wasting her energy trying to end her family home. They were too stubborn to listen to her anyway.

Back in the Chimera Ra paced across the black marble floor of Alaric's chamber, the flare of the candles barely noticeable compared to the incandescence of his male form. Alaric stood with his hip leaning against a large stone table covered with weapons. Up until a couple of chimes ago he too had been pacing so much he thought he would wear a pattern in the floor. The sun was setting and they were running out of time.

"He will go for the girl." Ra continued his pacing. "She is his connection to earth."

I am such a fool thought Alaric. "When this night is over I will step down and surrender myself for judgment."

That caught Ra's attention. He stopped pacing and spun around to face his high priest. "What are you talking about?" he demanded.

Alaric reached over the table and chose a long sword with a black blade. He took a few practice swings with it. He liked the weight of it, and the feel of it in his hand. "Stepping down. I cannot rule if I cannot see what is best for our people. And going to earth to sire a child definitely was not in the best interests of our people."

"You cannot."

"Beg your pardon?"

"You cannot. I do not allow it."

Alaric shook his head, his dark eyes serious as a heart attack as they met the glowing golden eyes of Ra. "It is my fault the seal was broken. You said it yourself. She is the connection. Her blood opened the door for his return."

Ra shrugged. " We all do things we regret. So we fix it."

"And how do we do that?" Alaric slid the sword into a scabbard at his hip. "I will not allow her to die. She is my daughter."

"There is no reason for her to die. The door is already open."

Twenty-Two

"Kamenwati." Alicia's voice was a husky whisper until she cleared her throat. "Kamenwati, I'd like you to meet my mother Jade Caer Wulfson." "Mom, Kamenwati Horakhty."

"As in…?"

Meeting the parents is not something that Kamenwati, as the son of the Sun God Ra ever expected to worry about. But here he was hoping the *Moarte* approved of him as a mate for her adopted daughter. Not that it would keep him away if she didn't, it just made things easier. Alicia loved her family. They were the reason she ran away to face her nightmares alone was a feeble attempt to protect them, just like she pushed him away in an attempt to protect him. "My father is Ra Horakhty."

Now that put a different spin on things, as well as helped to explain why the males wore fighting leathers, and were fully loaded with weapons. The Magi had taken the offensive the moment he sensed her presence. Was he protecting Alicia or Kamenwati? She would have guessed Kamenwati but couldn't forget that his fireball smothered out the instant Alicia appeared, and not because it came in contact with that shield the god son had thrown up around her.

It took Jade exactly two seconds from the moment Alicia poofed herself between Jade and the Magi to realize what her daughter had become. Had the Magi been sent to protect her? And if so who gave the order? And she hadn't missed the way Kamenwati was looking at her daughter. She had to get Alicia alone, but she couldn't forget protocol. One didn't piss off a god. Not if one wanted to keep all their body parts intact.

"I am pleased to make your acquaintance." Jade inclined her head slightly.

Alicia turned to Conall, as if only now realizing he was standing there. "This is Conall. He is," she hesitated only a moment, " a friend of Kamenwati's."

Friend or bodyguard?

Conall dipped his head in acknowledgement of the introduction, and wondered why Alicia hadn't told her mother that Alaric had sent him. He still couldn't believe it. Alaric and the *Moarte*. That explained keeping it secret. It explained a lot.

Conall started when he felt as much as heard the incredulous laughter licking at his brain, and the *Moarte*'s musical voice. *Not in this or any other lifetime Magi.*

Before he had a chance to react Alicia continued. " Jade saved me from the *vampire* ..." The word vampire had a guilty ring to it, after all that is what she was—vampire. She ignored the resounding *No* along with the other voice, the one that kept insisting, *yes. Call to me child. You are one of us.* She had thought it was her father's voice, but now she wasn't so sure.

Been there, done that, when I was young and too stupid to know better. Not happening again.

She wasn't really surprised when the voice took on the evil resonance of the Seeker. *You belong to me,* it screeched. *You will be mine.*

Something besides the voices warring in her head nibbled at her brain even while her hand went to her stomach to try to ease the butterflies that flocked there whenever the Seeker drew near. Something was off, but she couldn't figure it out. While she worried the problem with one part of her mind she continued the conversation.

"...That murdered my parents. She adopted me when I was eight." The soft look she gave Jade and the glow in her eyes said it all. Theirs was a connection just as strong, if not stronger than any blood connection.

A shadow passed over the sun and four pairs of eyes looked up. The air was stifling with nary a breeze to offer relief, and there was not a single cloud in the sky. The chickens had ceased scratching and decided it was time for a siesta, roosting in clumps of dried grasses at the base of trees and along the old rail fence along one side of the yard. Alicia shivered at the evil that crawled along the trail the sun left in its passage across the bright sky as if it were trying to hurry it along on its journey, as it paved the way for its master.

Jade felt like there was a blanket rubbing over her skin, its rough texture catching in the short hairs on her arms. Soon it would cover her head making it difficult to breathe. *Bring it on,* she thought. She had waited a long time for a shot at the unseen monster that chased her daughter from her home, and kept her away for far too long. Jade knew about the nightmares. In the beginning when the dark haired child screamed in the night Jade had held and comforted her long after she had fallen back to sleep muttering "*Don't move. He can't see you if you don't move.*" After several months the nightmares ended.

Then the child had grown into a beautiful young woman, and the nightmares returned. Jade knew exactly when that happened. Alicia might not scream in the night anymore, but the dark circles beneath her eyes, and the haunted look in their depth told the story. The hardest thing Jade was forced to do was allow her daughter the freedom to leave, study, and become the successful adult she was today.

Jade couldn't help her daughter then, but tonight she would not face her nightmare alone.

Magi. Jade knew there was something special about Alicia when she first saw her sprawled out like a sacrificial lamb, and heard her lost and alone searching for a mother who was no longer within her reach, while mourning a father she already knew was gone. She knew Alicia was a witch, which was why she believed the vampire was drawn to her in the first place. Her psychic ability would have been a beacon shining in the night to any of the undead within hearing, and anything else seeking more power. Althea had helped Alicia come to terms with her brush with the undead, and taught her how to hide her abilities so she did not unwittingly call out with them anymore. She learned so quickly, and was so brave in the face of danger, Jade couldn't be prouder if she had given birth to her.

Magi. The children of Ra. The chosen few who were given the powers of the Sun God, and then followed him beyond the heavens into the *Chimera* when he left the earth so many lifetimes ago. Unlike the vampire the magi were strongest during the daylight hours while they harnessed the power of the sun.

Jade's stomach growled.

"You are hungry," Kamenwati said. He stared into the passing sun as if they were communing, which they probably were. "We must eat."

Jade had to agree as another wave of hunger washed over her. She wondered if there was any chocolate in her back pack. Her owl had caught a couple of mice, and an iguana while it followed the trail Conall left, but that energy was pretty much gone. Too bad there wasn't a *MacDonald's* or a *Wendy's* handy. She could use a couple burgers and fries. "Sounds like a plan to me," she said. "Food. Lots of it. First I need a word with my daughter in private."

"Come inside, Mom." Alicia headed toward the small farmhouse, Jade followed, Kamenwati disappeared without stirring as much as a dust ball, and Conall eyed a couple of the fatter chickens that squawked as if they knew exactly what he was thinking.

Four wolves ran full out across the Mexican landscape not bothering to follow any road. Their beacon called to them across the vast land. They headed for one of their own, and each one would be able to find her no matter where she was. The smaller white female staggered, and two grey furred males immediately flanked her. She was exhausted and needed to feed before she collapsed, but she refused to show any sign of weakness.

They needed to reach their destination before it was too late. Suddenly the largest male veered from their path and headed northwest instead of due north. It wasn't their place to question their Alpha, so they turned as the well trained unit they were, and followed.

The wolves came up against a stone fence that surrounded a farmer's field, and stopped short. The wall was too tall for them to jump, and stretched as far as they could see. *Shit.* This was going to cause a delay they couldn't afford. It was bad enough his mate had sent them on this side trip. He would have denied her, except that he found it difficult to deny her anything she requested, except when he was positive it was not in her best interests. He hadn't wanted to make this side trip but she had insisted he find Matthew.

Over there. His bright yellow eyes spotted a break in the wall about a hundred yards to their right; the stone was crumbled enough they could easily make it over. They jumped the rubble, and resumed their full out run through the field, veering slightly to the left to make up for the detour. Ahead of them a farmer dressed in a white shirt and baggy brown trousers was holding the handles of a plow pulled by a mule. The mule caught the scent of the wolves and panicked.

The farmer fell back when the mule bolted, although it didn't make it very far with the heavy plow still attached. It stopped several feet ahead shivering and whimpering in terror. The farmer's own eyes grew like saucers when he spied the wolf pack heading for him at a dead run.

"Shit." He frantically looked around for some sort of weapon but all he saw were the acres of freshly tilled soil. He'd left his shotgun back at the house as usual. Wasn't his wife going to love this? She was always yapping at him to take his damn gun when he went to work in the fields but he never did. Why would he? In the fifty-one-years he'd been working the fields there had been no need for a gun. There had never been so much as a coyote come to raid the hen house, and now there were four fully grown wolves heading right for him.

Oh yes. Patricia was going to love being right. He could hear her now. "I told you to carry your gun. Why do you even have it? It's not like you ever use it. Do you even know if it works?" But wait. He wasn't going to get shit for leaving his gun behind. Hell, he wasn't going to get shit for anything anymore. He didn't have a chance against one full grown wolf while unarmed, never mind a whole damn pack He wondered what he would miss the most. Her harpy voice when she nagged him, which was most of the time, or the way her eyes softened when she didn't think he was looking.

The wolves were only ten feet away now. He should get up, make himself look larger, face them like a man. He sat where he was with freshly tilled soil stuck to the seat of his pants, hands and feet covered, too terrified to move. "I love you Patricia," he whispered. " I'm sorry I left you."

Hot tears splashed down his cheeks. Terror clamped its icy fingers around the heart that tried frantically to keep beating, and squeezed. The wolves were so close he could see their yellow eyes, and the bright orange eyes of the female. At the last possible second they veered to pass through the space between man and beast.

Relief didn't last a moment before the man grabbed his chest, and buckled over. Fifteen minutes later he woke to his wife's harpy voice; it was the most beautiful thing he'd ever heard. " Wake up you lazy lout. What's the idea of taking a nap in the middle of the day? The mule could have run off." Not that it would have got far with that plow dragging behind.

The farmer stared into the sky as a shadow passed over the sun, and shivered. He sat up, wrapped his arms around his wife who was kneeling beside him, and bawled his eyes out.

Lynn Marie Simpson

A few miles northwest of the farmer's field the wolf pack came to a skidding halt. A huge shaggy black wolf blocked their path, its paws the size of basketballs, and its teeth bared. Its shaggy fur gave it an unkempt, feral appearance, and its dark eyes glittered viciously. The white female staggered, shimmered, and shifted into its human form. As if by mutual agreement the males followed suit.

Twenty-Three

*C*ome *to me my children.* The Seeker called to
every vampire within migrating distance. The ground
roiled as if there was a great earth quake as the
vampires strained to escape their daytime prisons. As soon
as the sun set they would rise and continue the journey many
had begun the night before. En masse they travelled beneath
the earth following a need obey they could no more resist
than they could resist their need for blood.

Bring her to me.

Twenty-Four

Luke glared at the lobo that worked for Jade. Okay with Jade if you wanted to get technical, considering he headed up the Mexican division of O'Connor Search and Rescue, but Luke wasn't in the mood to be technical. The mere thought of Jade having anything to do with this lobo made him crazy. Jade was his. He was lycan, and lycans did not share—especially with a lobo. Lycans and lobos didn't mix well. Lycan were humans that shifted to wolves while lobos were wolves born with the ability to shift into human form. One could probably argue they were the same—wolf and human—but Luke wasn't about to argue that point either.

"What do you mean you won't take us?" Luke's voice was a low threatening growl in the back of his throat. He was

Alpha and did not take kindly to refusal of any kind, and especially not from a lobo.

"You heard me *lycan*. I am *not* taking you to that farmhouse."

They were facing off outside the house that was both the office of O'Connor S&R and Matthew's home. Although he was no longer in wolf form the hair on the back of his neck still bristled. He'd been feeling antsy for days, and it wasn't getting any better. Something big was going down. He could feel it in the air. Matthew trusted his instincts; instincts that were well honed after years of hunting with Jade. When he stepped off the porch to start his rounds and saw the lycans running across the yard he thought they were the cause of his unease, only now he wasn't so sure. That didn't mean he trusted those two unmated males anywhere near his female. He might be lobo but that didn't mean he was stupid, regardless of what the lycans thought.

The door behind him opened and Theresa stepped onto the porch, her hand hovering protectively over the slight swell in her abdomen. Matthew sucked his breath in sharply, tasting the unique scent of wildflowers that was hers, and the lust that rolled off the larger of the unmated males. He growled a warning, baring his teeth. Theresa stepped closer and placed a hand on his forearm, her smile secretive and meant for him alone. *Relax wolf. He is only a boy. You have nothing to worry about.*

Matthew's body relaxed beneath her soothing touch, but he did not relax his posture.

Jade's daughter, there was no mistaking for any other, except for the length of her hair and her diminutive size they could be twins, pushed aside her two burly brothers who were trying their best to block her from view, and snarled at them when they tried to restrain her. Once away from her brothers she didn't seem nearly so small. "Shove the testosterone boys before this becomes a useless free for all." She staggered slightly as if her own slight weight was too much for her legs to carry, and faced him.

Matthew bit back a smirk, no sense inciting the males when he was out numbered, besides Theresa was present and he wasn't about to risk her or their young.

"You too Matthew." She was so sick of their stupid petty prejudices and distrust. She got enough of that when they visited Willow Bend. Don't get her wrong, she loved the place, especially Mrs Gray and the Inner Sanctum, but the lycans didn't trust her or her mother any more than her father and brothers trusted Matthew, just because they were a little different. She was surprised they accepted Quinn and Gheorgès considering who their mother was, but Dad had been their Alpha, had led them to safety all those years ago, and they accepted his sons for that—besides they looked like him. Still, she had listened to enough garbage today, and Mom needed them whether she would admit it or not.

Ignoring the males Emerald smiled at Theresa, her face lighting up, and her eyes swirling with power. " Hi," she said in a gentle tone that held no detectable compulsion, and Matthew relaxed more. "You must be Theresa. We spoke on the phone several times."

" And there is no mistaking you. You look like your mother." Theresa stepped forward after first giving Matthew's forearm another gentle squeeze, and put her arm around Emerald's shoulders in a motherly fashion. " What is wrong with you men," she reprimanded. " Can't you see this poor girl is falling down on her feet?" Her voice was gentle but firm and Emerald liked her immediately. "I am pleased to finally meet you. Jade has spoken of all of you so often I feel like I know you already."

As Theresa steered Emerald toward the steps she glanced over at Luke. " By the way you look good without the beard Luke. Makes me wonder what you usually look like."

Matthew growled, and Luke looked distinctly uncomfortable. There was only one reason this female would mention his beard, Jade had talked to her. He rubbed the short dark stubble that shadowed his chin and hoped it would grow in soon. Gheorgès guffawed in the background, and Quinn managed to look anywhere rather than at their father. Luke bared his teeth at Gheorgès which only made him grin, and look unrepentant.

Maybe it's time to knock Gheorgès up the side of the head, Luke thought, *teach him who's Alpha around here.* He settled for a low warning growl, and this time Gheorgès had the good sense to look, if not completely remorseful, at least a little discomfited, and his grin disappeared.

Emerald and Theresa exchanged glances, and rolled their eyes. " Males," they said in unison.

A shadow passed over the sun, and Emerald had to force herself to stay where she was. Never before had she felt such a compulsion to take wing and fly. She needed to travel north, and she could only assume it was because her mother needed her. It wouldn't do to take flight and go, if she left the males alone she couldn't be sure they wouldn't come to blows. "Matthew." She wanted to compel the male to take them to the farmhouse but he was her mother's trusted friend, and she couldn't do that to him. She had to trust that he would do what he needed to do of his own free will. " What my father meant to say." She flicked her eyes at her father when she sensed him move behind her, and he stilled, but his voice rang in her head.

Do not apologize to this lobo.

Not once in her seventeen years had Emerald spoken back to or disobeyed her father but something was controlling her that she couldn't fight, and so she said. "Would you *please* take us to the old farmhouse? We were on our way when my mother requested we come here first. She mentioned a med kit. Do you know what she was talking about?"

Luke growled, but didn't say a word. He wasn't angry at his daughter for apologizing for him as much as he was angry at himself for letting his personal prejudice dictate his behavior. He was used to dealing with people, and the lobo should be no different than anyone else. What kind of leader couldn't deal?

Gheorgès was staring daggers in the back of her head, and Quinn was picturing Theresa sitting on a stool, her expression wistful, her hands covering her abdomen, sheltering the child nestled there. She wasn't surprised, Gheorgès was a warrior, and Quinn was an artist at heart. He could turn a bloody battlefield into a piece of art.

Matthew's thunderous expression softened, but he looked uncomfortable. "I cannot go to the farmhouse." His eyes shifted to Theresa's abdomen and back to Emerald. "I cannot leave my mate alone. You don't understand."

He was worried for Jade, "med kit" was a code they used when all hell was about to break loose, but he was terrified to leave his wife alone. For the past few nights he could sense the restlessness in the vampires, and last night he felt them getting closer. There was no violation of the law, no attacks on humans, nothing to betray their presence, but that didn't mean they were not here. Besides, Theresa was pregnant. He could not leave her to face the threat alone.

Emerald fought the need to leave. Her form wanted to shift, needed to shift, she could feel feathers poking beneath her skin. "I do understand. You are worried for Theresa and your young, which is as it should be. But we need to get to my mother. Can you at least give us the med kit, or tell us what it means?"

Theresa locked eyes with Matthew. "You must go Matthew," she said. " You owe it to Jade."

"Fine." Matthew didn't sound like it was fine. If anything he sounded like he wanted to mangle something.

Theresa smiled at her husband, and patted his arm as she led Emerald across the porch. "That's better. Now everyone come inside. I have lunch all ready and Emerald is not the only one who needs to eat."

Twenty-Five

Jade and Alicia sat at the small round wooden table that Alicia had so lovingly polished by hand. Alicia filled two tin cups with well water from the bucket on the counter, set them on the table, and then sat across from Jade. "I'd make tea but all I have is water. I haven't been to town to get anything yet."

Scattered images of a dark alley, head bent over a strange man, fangs elongated as hunger clawed at her insides haunted her. Did she really sink her fangs...even now she had trouble believing she had fangs...vampire. She had become the vilest of creatures. A monster, destined to survive from the innocent blood of others, their life's essence. But she *didn't* do it. She did not drink. She was stronger than that. She had sent the man away. She was not a monster. But she was a monster, wasn't she? She had fed from Kamenwati, drank from the vein that ran from his heart. When the power of his blood hit the back of her throat she'd felt more alive than she had in years. Strong...powerful...alive! She wanted to take every drop while she rode him like a bronco.

"Alicia, are you all right?" Jade reached across the table and placed her steady hand over Alicia's, which was shaking so badly the water in her cup was splashing over the rim.

Alicia jumped and blinked at Jade as if only just realizing she wasn't alone. "Yeah...um..." She swallowed, and cleared her throat. "I'm fine."

"You sure?" Jade tilted her head and watched her daughter with a critical eye.

Alicia patted her head. "What's the matter? Is my hair sticking straight up? Or maybe my fangs are showing just a tad too much," she added sardonically. She put her hand to her mouth and checked the tips of her teeth. "I know they're here," she mumbled with her finger in her mouth, moving her finger back and forth frantically, and hysteria making her voice rise. "They are right here." She caught her finger on the tip of one, and pulled back to stare at the tiny bubble of blood. Hunger was the demon that controlled her as fangs exploded. She stuck the finger in her mouth and sucked.

Minutes passed, or hours, or maybe it was only a moment. Alicia pulled her finger from her mouth and stared at it horrified by what had just happened. God, even her own blood was a trigger. The eyes she flickered toward Jade reflected her panic. Alicia swallowed once, twice, three times before she could force the dreaded question past the lump in her throat. "Will you destroy me like you destroyed the monster that killed my mama and papa?"

Jade lifted the tin cup to her lips and took a sip, not once losing eye contact. The water was warm, which wasn't surprising, but it was clear and refreshing. Chickens squawked in the yard, and Jade didn't miss the odor of burning feathers. She hoped the mage knew what he was doing because she would rather eat raw meat than meat that was overcooked. Maybe she was spoiled. Okay, she would admit it, she *was* spoiled. There were people in her life that enjoyed cooking for her, and because she loved to eat and couldn't boil water, she was more than willing to let them do so.

Across the table from her Alicia looked like a lost child, but there was a resolve in her dark eyes; she was determined to do whatever was necessary. "Do you remember the story the Children of Ra?" Jade asked.

Alicia blinked. Of course she remembered that story. She had been obsessed with the Sun God and his followers her entire life. She lived to prove the stories were true, that there really was a group of men that had become gods and followed Ra to live beyond the heavens. One of the reasons she wanted on that Egyptian dig, was so she could find evidence of their existence. "That was my favorite story. The reason I became an archaeologist, so I could prove the existence of the Children of Ra." Her forehead puckered, and her eyes narrowed. "Why are you bringing this up now?"

"The Children of Ra were priests chosen by Ra to gain immortality, and the powers of a god." Jade continued as if Alicia had not answered. Suddenly she reached across the table and clasped Alicia's hands. Their eyes locked, and Jade's swirled with power. "It will take too long to tell the story. It is easier to show you."

The room grew hazy and a movie began to play in Alicia's head. Her brows furrowed when she realized the men looked like her father—without fangs. She watched the scene play out before her.

Two men of identical dark looks and build entered the sacred chambers draped in white robes, and nothing else. Theron watched his brother beneath hooded eyes like a hawk watching his prey; his expression gave nothing away of his thoughts. Alaric was Ra's favorite and it made his blood boil. *Why did everyone favor Alaric?* Alaric had been their mother's favorite as well. Theron had only joined the priests of the sun because their mother had made such a fuss when Alaric had become a priest. But what did it get him? "It pleases me you are following your brother into the light," she had said in a tone that spoke volumes for her indifference to whether he became a priest or a stable boy. *Following his brother.* Theron nearly sneered at the memory, but caught himself just in time.

"Is something on your mind, brother?"

Alaric's solicitous voice grated on Theron, but he forced a small smile on his handsome face, and held his brother's eyes. "I was wondering why we have been summoned?"

"It is not our place to question our God."

Theron allowed his eyes to dip, more so Alaric would not be witness to the hatred that burned in his soul than in repentance. " Forgive me brother." Theron forced a hint of shame into his voice, and mentally rolled his eyes at his brother's gullibility. *Does the fool really think I care what he or anyone else expects of me?*

"There is no shame in curiosity." Alaric quickly said. He hated making his brother feel bad. His mother did enough of that. Since they were small boys Alaric considered it his duty to make up for the hurts inflicted on his twin by their mother's cruel neglect. He could not fathom the reason for her indifference towards Theron. They were twins, of the same build, of the same features, of the same voice. There were no differences, and yet their mother was cruelly callous in her treatment of Theron.

There was an explosion of light and Ra appeared before them, a shimmering image of a man. They watched silently as the image solidified, and became corporeal. Ra stepped forward holding a golden chalice with the fiery sun emblazoned on the side. The twins bowed before their God and kept their eyes respectfully lowered.

"Raise thine eyes." Ra's voice boomed in the large chamber; it echoed off the stone walls like thunder over a mountain.

Four identical black eyes lifted to land on Ra's glowing form. "I offer a gift."

Theron fumed inwardly when Ra offered the chalice first to his brother, although it did not surprise him, only confirmed what he already knew- Alaric was Ra's favorite, just like he had always been their mother's. With no outward signs of emotion he accepted the chalice gracefully when offered. The glowing liquid inside had a slight coppery taste.

"You are the chosen." Ra's voice thundered around them, over them, through them. "My children. With this offering I bestow strength, wisdom, the power of the universe, and eternal life to you and all that come after you."

Agony struck with the viciousness of a she-bear defending her cubs. The twins doubled over clutching their abdomens. They walked through an eternity of flames as their human bodies were burned away, leaving behind a vessel capable of containing the powers of the universe.

Hours, days, or maybe only moments passed, there was no way to be sure. Time stood still while the brothers fought for survival. When it was finally over, they were no longer the young men who stepped into the sacred chamber. They stood taller, more powerful, the hunger in their bellies reflected in the dark orbs of their eyes.

Alaric and Theron stood and faced Ra, their lips parting to reveal long, sharp fangs. And so the Magi were born.

Alicia gasped, and pulled her hands away to end the vision. Her tongue toyed with the tips of her own fangs, and the hunger eating at her insides reflected that she felt in the vision. She swallowed convulsively several times, and took a deep breath. *How could this be? How could Ra create a race of monsters?* "What happened?" she finally whispered.

Jade reached out to scan their surroundings. Some of the chickens had settled back in their roosts, while others were once again scratching at the barren earth. The mage was in the orchard searching for edible fruit, and the godson had not yet returned. She reached further and found Luke and her triplets with Matthew. They weren't more than a couple hours away.

I love you. She sent the message across the miles, and quickly closed her mind. She could feel Luke there, he was always there, hovering, as much a part of her as she was of him, inseparable—but she could not allow a stronger connection at this time. It was not safe, not when the enemy hovered so near. Jade sighed inaudibly. If she had her way she would lock her entire family up where they would be safe, but she was *Moarte* and they were Lycan, and neither species were ever truly safe. And now there were Magi to contend with, and their dark sides. The only way for Alicia to face her nature, and her future, was to first know the past.

She had been heading in that direction from early in life, and now it was up to Jade to help her get there.

"Theron was not satisfied with what he had been given. He was weak, and unable to control his impulses."

Lies. Do not listen to the Moarte. She spouts lies. Alicia ignored the voice in her head that was growing stronger, and concentrated on what her mother was saying.

"...he wanted more power. He wanted to be a god. Like many cultures he believed you gained the strength of your enemy by consuming a part of them. He was obsessed with the need for power. He kept his desires well hidden, a priest by day...a beast by night." Jade reached her palms out and waited. Alicia hesitantly placed her own palms on top, and the movie continued.

Theron was watching the girl down by the river as she beat some clothing against one flat rock with another in an attempt to clean them. The way her slim body was bent over made an inviting offer. He wanted her. He had for months, even before the change, and now the need to take her, all of her, was excruciating. He wanted to be in her while he took her blood into himself. His cock stirred, stiffened, pushed at its restrictions as it sought the source of its distress.

Theron approached the girl on silent steps. When he was almost upon her something gave his presence away, and she jumped covering her rapidly beating heart with one delicate hand. When she realized it was only the priest, her pink lips turned up in a relieved smile. "You near gave me a heart attack," she said in a soft voice. "You should not sneak up on a person like that."

Theron took another step closer to the trusting girl. He loved being a priest. Everyone went out of their way to do a priests' bidding, after all he was their voice to the gods.

When Theron was close enough to smell the hot spice of her blood, he smiled, revealing his fangs for the first time. Fear flashed in the girls blue eyes, and her heart began to pump that delicious blood faster. " Offer yourself to me, child." Theron's voice was both evil and seduction at the same time. The girl wanted to scream. She wanted to run. Theron read her thoughts as easily as if they were his own, but he held her in his steady gaze.

" Offer yourself," he demanded. A wicked smile played over his lips as the female slipped her shift from her shoulders.

"The rush of human blood was incredible, intoxicating, addicting, and like any drug the rush soon wore off leaving Theron needing more." Jade's voice was a whisper in her mind even while Alicia watched Theron with the female he had chosen, unable to tear her hands away to end the vision.

"Theron drained the female and hid the body, but he was a smart man and realized it wouldn't be long before she was missed. He went back to the village and planted a false memory in her father's mind of an argument between them involving a village boy. When his daughter did not return from the river he went to search for her. Finding nothing but the abandoned wash he assumed she ran off with her lover. Theron was more careful after that. He convinced Ra and his brother that it would be a good idea if he were to build a new temple of worship in a far away country. Ra already had worshippers around the world, but he jumped at the chance to rid himself of the dark-souled one. Overnight a new Temple of the Sun appeared in a small Mayan village. The villages accepted the appearance of the temple without question, after all, Ra was a very powerful God and if he wished to have a temple he would have a temple.

"Theron used his newly developed gifts to convince the villagers to send their young daughters to be sequestered at the Temple where they would devote their lives to Ra. It was a perfect arrangement. The villagers willingly turned over their females, and Theron had an unending supply of victims to feed both his carnal appetite, and that for blood, but he soon realized that human blood was not powerful enough to sustain him for long, and he needed more."

Jade paused to take a sip of the tepid water. "In the meantime Ra's magi grew in number as he offered his *gift* to those he deemed worthy. His misgivings about Theron were forgotten the moment he sent the priest away. When it came to the dark one 'out of sight out of mind' was how Ra looked at it. As long as he didn't have to see the man he didn't care what Theron did.

"Ra should have been more careful. While his priests were sleeping peacefully one night Theron travelled through the Chimera to sneak into the Temple and steal the sacred chalice from under their noses. The chalice held the essence of life, the means of converting more of his kind. Theron knew he had to work quickly before the priests woke with the dawn and discovered their loss. Theron hurried back to his temple intending to force his novices to drink from the chalice. He believed that by converting the novices he would enhance the power in their blood thereby giving him what he craved."

Theron unlocked the massive wooden door and entered his temple. *His temple.* He still couldn't believe how simple it had been to convince the villages that he was the Sun God. None had actually seen Ra and so it was as simple as performing a few parlor tricks, and

177

they were all over themselves trying to please him. Such feeble minds—so easy to manipulate. Only the chosen were allowed entrance to the Temple, and the villagers didn't know that once the novices entered the temple they left their lives behind—literally. If anyone made it past the door they entered a huge empty chamber with symbols of the sun god embellishing the walls, ceilings, and floor. What they couldn't see was the secret door beneath the sun that led to the real place of worship.

Theron stepped on the edge of the sun that adorned the center of the floor, and shuddered at the revulsion that raced through him. The symbols of Ra, although abhorrent to him were a necessary evil should anyone make it past his wards. The center of the sun rose and Theron stepped onto the dark stain covered platform that rose beneath it. The platform descended to the darkness below and he listened for the frightened whimpers of his chosen. It was music to his ears, and an adrenaline rush to his soul. The platform stopped. It was dark, but Theron did not need any artificial light to see. He surveyed his place of worship, and his dark eyes glittered with anticipation.

He stood in a large circular chamber surrounded by several small doors with small slits that he opened to reveal the occupants. Behind each heavy door was a small four by four chamber with cold, damp stone walls. These were where his chosen rested while they waited their turn.

The center of the room, the spot directly beneath the painting of the sun on the main floor, was stained dark with blood and other bodily fluids. This was his domain where he had discovered a new high—fear. The scent of their fear strengthened him and fear-enhanced blood was a powerful aphrodisiac. It was to this spot he brought the novices of his temple and taught them what their devotion meant to him. This was where he took their lives to replenish his own.

There were four metal rods hammered into the stone floor with a length of chain fastened to each hook. These he used to immobilize the novices. Theron could have used his powers to enthrall them and keep them immobilized but he found that if he did that it not only immobilized them, it held their fear at bay, and he thrived on the fear he could instill in them.

The vision flashed from the center of the chamber to the interior of one of the darkened cells, and the image of Theron changed to that of a young female.

Sangria shoved at the heavy wooden door but it didn't budge. Her fingers were torn and bloody by the time she finished systematically searching every inch of the walls that she could reach. Nothing. The cell was empty, and silent now except for her own shallow breathing, the whisper of her footsteps, and the scratching of her nails along the stone surface. She couldn't hear her sisters breathing, or their fearful whimpers, which was both terrifying and a relief.

Had it only been two days since her father brought her to the temple? It seemed like a thousand years since she had begged him to take her back home with him, and he had refused her pleas. Her mother was dead, and her father did not like the way the village boys watched her since she began to fill out like a woman should. She understood his reasoning, he believed he was doing what was best for her, but the moment she set foot on the stone steps leading to the temple door she could feel bugs crawling over her skin, and a shadow passed over her soul.

Her father told her she was being childish, kissed her goodbye, and shoved her through the temple door when it suddenly opened. Sangria knew her father loved her, but he did not understand the feelings she sometimes got, and he believed the only safe place for her was in the temple. Her service to God would save her soul.

Sangria wasn't so sure, but she loved her father and did not want to cause him any more concern than she already had. She had trembled as she stumbled into the larger chamber, but she refused to give in to the impulse to turn and run. *The next time she would obey her impulses. If there ever was a next time.* Although the inner chamber was decorated the same as any other temples she had ever been in, it *felt* wrong.

The heavy door to the outer chamber closed behind her with an audible click, and Sangria felt as if someone had cut off her air supply. A robed figure suddenly appeared beside her, and nudged her toward the large sun in the center of the chamber. Already off balance by the sudden appear of what Sangria assumed was a priest, she stumbled and nearly fell, catching herself just as the floor began to move. Sangria shuffled backward but Theron grabbed her roughly by the arms and pushed her onto a platform covered with dark stains that stopped in front of them.

The moment she touched the platform with her bare feet she gasped and nearly doubled over. The image that came to her was so strong there was no escaping it. It was a girl from their village who had been Sangria's friend up until she entered the temple a couple of months ago. She was laying spread eagle on the platform, held immobilized by heavy chains while a male ravaged her. Sangria watched helpless as he sank his fangs into her neck. It seemed like hours had passed before her body quit struggling, and her screams grew silent, then the man lifted his head and looked right at Sangria.

The priest.

Theron dragged Sangria from the platform and threw her into this barren cell. How long ago was that? It must have been hours ago. Although there was no light in this hellhole she could sense the rising of the sun on the surface. Sangria clawed frantically at the wooden door desperate to be gone before that monster came back for her.

Help me, she pleaded silently. *If anyone is out there please help me.*

Almost as if someone had heard her anxious pleas the cell door was flung open, and Sangria staggered into the main chamber, stopping short when she saw the priest standing in the center of that cursed platform, surrounded by images of the dead, and holding a shimmering golden chalice. His hood had fallen off and his fangs were clearly visible when he spoke.

"My child." Theron spoke in a quiet, soothing voice that belied the monster she now knew him to be. "You look distressed. Are your accommodations not to your liking?"

The priest acted as if he was truly a god, and she was simply a novice in his temple. Sangria blinked against the light coming from the golden chalice, so bright in the dark chamber that it nearly hurt her eyes, and watched the priest warily. "Where are my sisters?" she demanded.

Theron's eyes narrowed, and he frowned at her. "Do you dare to question me?"

Sangria's head shook rapidly, and she lowered her gaze submissively while keeping a wary eye on her captor. She had to figure a way out of here before she ended up like her friend. "Forgive me," she whispered. "I have no wish to offend. I was merely curious as to the whereabouts of my sister novices."

Theron waved his hand and several cell doors flew open. Sangria watched as the occupants of the cells walked with jerky movements to the open doorways to stand and stare at Theron with lifeless eyes.

"As you can see your sisters are quite happy here."

Not exactly you monster. Her childhood friend was not present among the living, rather she was hovering on the edge of the sacrificial platform a mere specter of her former self, and none of the other zombie like women seemed happy either.

As Sangria watched with narrowed eyes, Theron beckoned each of the females to him. They approached on jerky, unstable gaits like puppets with no will of their own.

Stop! The word sprang to mind but Sangria could not push it past a throat blocked by some unseen hand. One by one her sisters accepted the golden chalice from the priest, and drank. When it was Sangria's turn she found the will to turn her head, but Theron's hand snaked out and wrenched it back so he could pour the golden liquid down her throat. Sangria was surprised by the coolness of the liquid that came from the glowing chalice. It was cool and sweet as it trickled down her throat but the moment it hit her stomach it started to burn. Sangria clutched her abdomen and keeled over in her own agony as the screams of her sisters filled the air.

Even as the agony that ripped through Sangria and her sisters ripped through Alicia the vision changed, and they were once again in Ra's temple where the priests were rising with the dawn.

The priests entered the sacred chamber to offer their morning devotions to Ra, and froze in shocked disbelief. The stone altar was empty. The golden chalice was gone. The chamber was completely empty except for the altar so it was easy to see that the chalice had not simply fallen.

Their first thought was they had somehow offended Ra and the god had taken their source of life away. Hunger gnawed at their bellies making it hard to think, and images of fangs sinking deep into human throats as they drank their fill haunted their thoughts. They had no way of knowing that Theron had figured out how to send his own desires into their minds, making them desire things they wouldn't normally consider. Nobody except Alaric had even given Theron a second thought since his exile. The graphic images coupled with their desire to survive soon proved too powerful for some of the magi who attempted to leave the temple in search of prey.

Alaric stepped between the magi and door to the temple, and tried to reason with them. "Ra did not do this," he insisted. "This is the work of another." He did not tell them that he could smell his twin all over the room; a scent that shouldn't be there considering Theron had not set foot in the temple for months. "I can return the chalice to its rightful place," he assured them.

The group nearest to him pushed him aside, and the starvation that rolled off them, and glittered in their eyes giving them an inhuman appearance took Alaric aback. *How was it possible they were so hungry? He also felt the need to feed but it did not dominate him.*

"You can get nothing back," they threw at him. " Ra has abandoned us. We will not just sit here and die."

Alaric pulled himself to his greatest height, and puffed out his chest much like a bird trying to show he was bigger and stronger than he really was. "You will not leave this temple." He could read their thoughts, and knew they were intent on feeding off the humans. He would not allow this. He could not allow this. They were not animals without thought or reason. Ra had given them a gift, and they would learn to live with it.

Alaric willed the door to shut. The magi turned on him and snarled. Alaric faced the row of fangs in front of him and wondered if he had the strength to keep them in check. *Where are you Ra? I could use some help right about now.*

" Open this door and move out of our way," they demanded.

" Give me a chance to prove that Ra did not take the chalice," he almost pleaded. " I know you are hungry. I also am hungry, but we cannot give in to our baser needs and simply feed on the villages. Think about it. They will hunt us down and destroy us like the animals we would become."

Several magi had taken position at his back, and Alaric hoped they were for him, and not against him.

He was relieved when one of them spoke from his position behind him.

"Alaric is right," he said. "If we go out into the village and feed they will destroy us. I know you want to. I want to. I can picture it in my head as clearly as if I had done it a hundred times, but that does not make it right."

"Ha," spat a mage. "We are much more powerful than the humans. They cannot harm us."

"You are being foolish my brother," another mage said. "Give Alaric the chance to bring the chalice back."

There was a blast of light and the mage was thrown back as the door to the temple blew open.

The visions were jumping around so much now that Alicia had the beginnings of a headache, but still she clasped Jade's hands, afraid she would miss something important.

Poison! Sangria could not believe the priest had poisoned them all, even as she clutched her stomach in a futile attempt to squelch the inferno growing there as the poison ate away her insides. It seemed like hours had passed in agony before the screams of her sisters died away to whimpers, and then silence as they exhaled their last breaths. Sangria was dying too. She knew it as well as she knew her own name. She could sense the priest moving amongst the bodies of her sisters but did not have the strength to open her eyes to track his whereabouts. It didn't really matter anyway. She was dying and he could do nothing more to her.

Theron could not believe it. *Dead. They were all dead.* Angry he grabbed the female nearest him and threw her limp body against the cold stone of the wall.

It hit with a satisfying 'splat' and he threw another, and another, but soon that was not satisfying enough. *This was all Ra's fault. Ra had tricked him into destroying his children and he in return would destroy Ra's children. Every breathing one of them.* He was so angry when he stepped onto the platform and willed it to rise that he did not realize one female still breathed. Already he could feel the magi's hunger and he played on that.

Sangria winced each time a sister's body hit a wall. She tried to judge where in the chamber the priest was, and when it would be her turn. Suddenly he stopped his rampage. Sangria listened to his steps as he grew nearer to her. She bit her tongue to keep from making a sound, and willed herself to stop breathing when his foot came out and kicked her in the ribs, before stepping on the platform and rising to the surface. She sighed with relief when the platform returned empty. Sangria waited for several long minutes after she sensed the priest leaving the temple completely before she dragged her weakened and bruised body across the floor and onto the platform.

"Rise," she whispered but the platform did not move. Sangria could not help herself. She began to sob in desperation, and willed the platform to rise and take her from this hellhole. *Please do not make me die down here.*

The platform began to rise.

The godson was back from wherever he ventured. Jade could feel his power boost her own, and the visions became more intense. Alicia had a death grip on her hands, and although her own shook uncontrollably, Alicia did not release the vision.

The door to the temple blew inward knocking those closest back into the room. Theron stood outlined in the doorway, the morning sun surrounding him like a halo. While the magi stared in startled surprise at the intruder, he dragged forward two struggling humans that were bleeding from wounds on their necks. "I brought breakfast," he taunted and tossed the frightened humans into the mob of hungry magi.

The scent of fresh blood was too powerful to ignore. Chaos erupted. Magi fell upon the screaming humans like a pack of wild dogs on a deer carcass ruled by blood lust. Fangs pierced the veins on their necks, arms, and legs. They tore the humans apart in the frenzy before they ever bled out.

Alaric knew there was no way to control the blood-crazed mob, and still he fought to save the humans. At least not all the magi had succumbed to Theron's temptation, and those that remained in control fought alongside Alaric. There were too many now crazed, and those in control were too few.

The battle raged on for hours, soon turning to one of magic. Lightning struck at the temple as the magi attempted to blast each other. The battle escaped the confines of the temple and continued on into the village. The humans came to see what was causing all the commotion, and those controlled by the blood lust fell upon them.

Ra was enraged by what was occurring. The fates had warned him about toying with creation, but had he listened? No. He crossed over from his home in the Chimera and faced Theron who had grown very powerful, but not yet as powerful as the god. With a blast of energy that nearly destroyed the entire village,

Ra threw Theron into the shadows between the Chimera and Earth where he would not be able to take on corporeal form during daylight hours. Those magi who had fought to protect the sanctity of his temple and his followers he offered to take with him into the Chimera were he resided. While many of the magi decided to follow Ra into the Chimera there were those who chose to stay on earth to hunt down and destroy the betrayers. Alaric wanted to stay on earth as well, to protect the humans from the nightmare his brother unleashed on them. Ra refused him. Alaric was his high priest, and as such he would become the Prince of the Magi and live in the Chimera. Theron accepted Ra's decree, believing he would better serve his god by fighting by his side in the Chimera to keep Theron from returning to earth.

The Fates were so angry with Ra for creating this new race of beings that they cursed them all. As long as they remained on earth they would require blood for their survival. They would crave it. The craving would never end, and those who chose to take a human life in order to prolong their own would forsake the warmth of the sun.

And so they became known as vampires.

The Fates must have a cruel sense of humor because they allow this new species to procreate. They bestow the offspring with special gifts, which are also a curse because they make them targets for those seeking more power. Once they reach the age of maturity which is about twenty-five years, the transition from human to mage takes place. If they survive the transition then the battle for their souls begins in earnest.

The visions dried up, and the two of them sat in the tiny kitchen. A grackle whistled in a tree outside, and a rooster crowed in reply. The aroma of cooking chicken reached their noses. Alicia looked at Jade. "What am I?" she asked. "Am I vampire or am I magi?"

Jade's lips curved into a cooked grin, and she winked. "You are what you have always been. Alicia Martinez Wulfson. My daughter."

Twenty-Six

Across an ocean, Megan watched the dark shadow drift across the sky, and started to sob. Her heart feeling like it was suddenly caught in a vice grip, Molly scooped her sobbing daughter, and didn't stop running until they were safe inside the inn with her back leaning against the closed door. It was several long minutes before her heart settled into its regular routine.

Twenty-Seven

The jeep bumped along the dirt road sending dust and rocks flying in its wake. Emerald's knuckles were white on the roll bar, and it had nothing to do with the drive. Caught in a vision shared by her mother and sister, she was not aware of the way her oversized brothers crowded her on the seat, but she was fully aware of the pain and suffering of each of the victims in the vision. She felt their pain as if it were her own. She shared their pain with her sister, and still it was overwhelming.

The vision ended with a snap, much like it would if the film on an old fashion movie reel broke, and Emerald collapsed against her brothers who had shifted her nearly off the seat.

"Hey," Gheorgès complained. " Get off me." He tried to push her forward but she shifted so she was leaning almost completely on him, and barely on Quinn.

"Welcome back baby sister." Quinn ducked when her small fist shot out at his head. " Hey," he pretended to whine. " Dad. She tried to hit me."

Emerald rolled her eyes, and smacked her back hard against Gheorgès, settling against his chest with a satisfied smirk when he finally gave in and wrapped his arms around her.

"Look who's being a baby," she teased Quinn. " Crying to his daddy cause a girl hit him."

"Hey. Technically you didn't hit me," Quinn managed to sound offended by the mere thought that a girl could hit him. "You missed."

" Whatever." Emerald rolled her eyes and sighed, silently thanking her brother for trying to distract her.

In the front seat, Luke growled low in his throat, and the back seat rumbled with laughter. " See what you have to look forward to," he said with a wink at Matthew. " With kids you get no respect."

Everyone was feeling a whole lot more relaxed after sharing the excellent meal Theresa prepared, and Luke had to admit that he liked the lobo in spite of himself. He should have known he would, Jade was an excellent judge of character and she loved the lobo, acted as if he was a member of her family, and in a way he was. The two of them went back many years.

Luke listened to the banter of his children in the backseat and wondered how they had grown up so fast. One moment he was holding all three in his powerful arms, the next they were fully grown Lycans.

Quinn eyed his sister now settled against their brother's broad chest. Outwardly, she appeared calm and relaxed, but every male in the jeep felt the turmoil inside her. " Seriously sis," he said watching closely for a sign she might try to weasel her way out of an answer. " What did you see?"

Emerald shrugged, and pulled Gheorgès arms tighter around her, uncaring if Gheorgès felt her shaking. She needed the comfort. *What did she see? What exactly were they heading toward?* For the first time since their father had ordered Daniel to return them to Mexican soil, she almost wished they had obeyed their mother and returned home.

The sudden need to reach her mother had her leaning into the front seat. " Can you make this thing go any faster, Matthew."

Matthew gave the jeep a shot of gas and it leapt forward spraying more dust and stone in its wake. The jeep bounced over a rise and stopped. Below them lay the farm. The small house and barn was in need of repair, the orchard beside the barn looked like it had once been tended by loving hands, even now the branches were hanging with ripe undersized fruit, but it was easy to see it had long been neglected. There were several chickens. Some were scratching at the bare earth digging up insects for their dinner, while others roosted lazily along an old rail fence.

The yard was otherwise deserted but every one of them in the jeep knew Jade was in that small house. They could feel her presence as easily as they felt the presence of Alicia and the other two men. As easily as they felt their presence, they could also tell there was no immediate danger. The air was hot with a hint of sulfur. Emerald stiffened, and Luke growled a warning low in his throat. Matthew lifted one brow, and Emerald leaned forward to place her small hand on her father's powerful shoulder.

" Be calm father," she counseled.

Luke's head whipped around and his dark eyes locked with his daughter's amber ones. The moment their eyes met, he felt the connection he was missing in his mind.

Do not come rushing in here all macho and stupid my love. The teasing lilt of his mate's voice whispering in his mind both calmed him and brought a tightening to his groin. He wanted to reach out to her, demand to know what was going on, but he knew it would be useless to try when Jade locked him out. He had learned to live with it, but that did not mean he liked it. That she could not keep him completely from her, or vice versa, was his only consolation. That tiny connection was the only thing that kept him sane when he thought she might be in danger.

Luke sighed, and while he didn't exactly relax, he did calm down. His gaze searched the lay of the land. There was a buzzing by his ear and he gave the obnoxious mosquito a satisfying swat. The small farmhouse looked vulnerable sitting in the open, but on the other hand, they would be able to see any approach, at least by road. He needed to check the back of the house for windows.

He made to get out of the jeep when his daughter once again stilled him merely by placing her much smaller hand on his shoulder. "Let me dad," she said.

Before he could answer, a small grackle took shape and flew from the back seat toward the farmhouse.

"Damn. I hate it when they do that."

Twenty-Eight

Jade felt the presence of the rest of her family on the road above the farmhouse, and her lips curved into a secretive smile. Her eyes met Alicia's, and she nodded. She watched the way Alicia placed her hand on Kamenwati's arm, and the godson smiled indulgently at her. There was no hiding what he felt for her daughter, and Jade relaxed. He would not be a problem. It was the mage she was concerned with.

Conall suddenly felt as if every fiber of his being was on high alert. Someone was approaching. He knew the moment the jeep stopped at the top of the hill leading to the farmhouse. He let his senses roam. It was easy to identify the four wolves that occupied the vehicle, but the fifth occupant was more of a challenge. She was hidden to him.

Until she spoke.

The moment his mind heard the female speak his entire body tensed. *Speak,* he urged with his mind. He needed to hear that voice again. Just the sound, as soft as velvet and as strong as steel caused a stir in his blood he had not felt in a very long time. Maybe never. *Say something. Anything,* he pleaded.

Let me dad.

Those three simple words had his pulse racing. His mind's eye searched for the source of the voice, but the jeep sitting atop the hill only held the four wolves.

Where was she?

A grackle whistled from the orchard. There was an answering whistle from behind the house. Conall's head whipped around. *There you are.* His lips curled into a smug grin.

Emerald landed in the sagebrush behind the house and reached out with her senses the way her mother taught her. The power emanating from the farmhouse was both awe inspiring, and a little bit terrifying. It was easy to locate her mother. Her essence was as familiar to her as her own. Emerald could have located her mother anywhere on the planet. The family had an unbreakable connection. Luke's was the strongest because he was her mate. He would follow her into the afterlife and fight to bring her back, such was the connection. One day Emerald hoped to have a love like that; someone who would keep her heart safe.

One day far away. Right now she was young and having way too much fun flirting with the boys back home, and driving her brothers crazy. They were probably the main reason she enjoyed flirting so much because the boys back home were definitely not exciting enough to bother with on their own, but the way Gheorgès, and even Quinn, puffed up like blow fish in an attempt to frighten them off was absolutely hilarious. One day she might get annoyed with their over protectiveness but right now she was young enough to enjoy it.

Emerald felt her mother's comforting presence like strong arms wrapped around her. Jade knew she was here, and was letting her know it. She could feel the presence of others in the room and tried to distinguish who they were. Alicia was one, although there was something different about her, and two males. The small grackle quaked under the heavy weight of the malevolent air that seemed to be closing in on it. Emerald tried to pinpoint the source of the evil but it was too elusive. The only thing she could tell for sure was that it was not coming from inside the farmhouse.

She was focusing on the farmhouse when her little bird heart began to beat erratically, fear overworking it until she worried it would cease to beat entirely. A grackle whistled a warning from the orchard, and Emerald returned the whistle in acknowledgement.

There you are.

The words startled the small grackle. It shot from the safety of the sagebrush in a flurry of feathers. Emerald was safely back at the jeep before she realized there was no evil intent in the voice she heard, only smug satisfaction.

Idiot. Not only did you not conceal your presence you ran like a scared rabbit. Emerald berated herself while she scanned her immediate surroundings for the presence of danger. The ominous cloud still hung in the air, and seemed to be gathering around the farmhouse, but it didn't look like anyone, or anything, had tracked her back to her family. Still she knew that their presence was already known and the advantage of surprise was lost.

Emerald shifted as she landed, and stood in front of the jeep dressed in a snug black tank top and dark blue jeans, her breath coming in short gasps while she tried to still the beating of her heart. She shook her long white blonde hair with its streaks of silver and gold so it settled around her shoulders and down her back. Scooping it back with hands that shook slightly she began to pleat it into a long braid that would hang to just below her shoulder blades. The familiar motion calmed her even further. Jade had wanted Emerald to cut her hair when she was still a child, still haunted by the death of her own mother caused by a vampire using her hair against her. But Emerald loved it long and flowing, and after many tears on Emerald's part Jade had conceded and allowed it to remain long, insisting that Emerald learn to use her hair to her advantage.

"There are two small windows, probably bedrooms," she finally said. She finished the brain and snapped her head to the left, sighing with satisfaction when her braid snapped to the right stopping short of slapping her in the face. A flick in the opposite direction, and then over her head, and Emerald faced her father.

Luke watched his daughter in silence, used to her ways. Gheorgès checked the knife tucked in his black motorcycle boot, and Quinn exchanged his button down shirt for a snug fitting t-shirt that showed off his muscles. Matthew stood beside the jeep, his hands on the roll bar, and watched the Wulfson family get ready to do battle. Although he would not admit it to anyone, he envied them their closeness, and hoped one day to have a large family with Theresa. Unease coursed through him at the thought of his mate all alone tonight. He did not know about the others, but he could feel the evil growing in the air around them with each passing moment

Do not worry my love. I've bolted the doors and retreated to the safe room. Theresa's soft voice was a comfort in the back of his mind. He loved her so much. Too much he sometimes thought, not knowing how he would survive without her.

I feel the same way Matthew. Be safe and do not worry about us.

I love you.

Right back at you. There was a heartbeat of silence, and then Matthew heard. *Hurry home. I miss you already.*

Luke finally broke the silence. " Are you expecting trouble daughter?"

Emerald shrugged. "There are two unidentified males in there."

"Males as in non-humans?" Gheorgès growled.

Emerald knelt down to tie a lace that had come undone in her runners. " Definitely non-human."

Quinn stepped forward and put a hand on Em's shoulder encouraging her to rise, and offering silent support. " Are they a threat to Mom or Alicia?" He asked the question that was on everyone's mind.

Emerald rose and faced her brother. Quinn always seemed to know when she felt inadequate and was always ready to lend his support. Only one of the many reasons she loved him so dearly.

"I don't think they are a threat," she said hesitantly. "For some reason I think they are supposed to help. At least I get the feeling they are here to protect Alicia. The rest of us, I'm not so sure about."

Luke faced the farmhouse anxious to reunite with his mate. He wanted to reach out to her but knew it would not be a good idea. She already knew he was here, and by reaching out he might just blow any advantage they had. "If you are ready," he said. " Let's go."

All five climbed back into the jeep, and Matthew turned into the dirt path to the farmhouse at a much slower pace.

When they neared the house the door opened and Jade stepped into the yard. Alicia appeared behind her, but hesitated when she saw them.

Emerald had no such hesitancy. She leapt from the jeep and rushed up the steps. "Hi Mom," she said on the way by. When she reached Alicia she wrapped her arms around her older sister. She didn't let go until Alicia relaxed and returned the hug. "I missed you so much Alicia. Why did you run away? Don't you know we all love you? Gheorgès was frantic."

Quinn reached his sisters in two strides and clasped Alicia close. Then he held her back to satisfy himself she was unharmed. He could see the changes in her. The pale hollow cheeks, the dark shadows under her eyes, the way she smiled without showing her teeth. He kissed her on the cheek. "Happy Birthday, Sis." He winked at her. "If I were as old as you I might not want to celebrate either."

Gheorgès pulled Alicia into a bear hug the second he got the chance, and glared at Emerald. "She's right you know," he said to Alicia. " We have all been very worried about you."

Tears pooled in Alicia's eyes. She missed her family so much, and was both torn and delighted that they were all here. *What will they see when they look at me?*

We will see our sister, the triplets answered together.

Gheorgès still had Alicia clasped in a bear hug and was swinging her around when a tall man clad in black leathers pants, motorcycle boots, and a black leather vest stepped through the doorway. The only visible weapon was the morning star idly swinging from one huge hand.

"Is that a morning star?" Gheorgès dropped Alicia so fast she stumbled and would have fallen if the huge male had not snagged out a hand to steady her.

The man's golden orbs shot daggers at Gheorgès despite the forced smile on his otherwise somber features. To his right, and slightly behind him stood another male. This one was a few inches shorter than the first. He was also clad in black leathers and motorcycle boots, but this male was definitely armed. There were knives tucked in his boots, and Gheorgès could clearly see the hilt of a sword hanging from his back.

Twenty-Nine

Kamenwati stepped through the door to find Alicia in the arms of another male, and saw red. It didn't matter that the male was her brother he still wanted to blast him into another universe. The only thing stopping him was Alicia. Any blast he let go now would be sure to fry her too. He pasted a smile he didn't feel on his lips, all the while shooting daggers at the couple.

Relax he told himself sternly. *This is her family.*

The male holding Alicia saw him and let go of her so suddenly she stumbled and would have fallen if Kamenwati had not reached out to steady her. He could kill the male for risking injury to his … *his what*? The thought was staggering. He had to assure his place in her life before it was too late, and he lost her.

What had the male said? Something about the morning star swinging at his side. Kamenwati stilled the weapon. Alicia laughed, and Kamenwati's eyes softened, the red veil of rage dissipating.

"If you hurt my sister you will deal with me."

The deep male grumble drew Kamenwati's attention from Alicia, and he actually smiled. The male was just a boy, albeit a very large, very muscular boy, and that he loved Alicia enough to threaten him only earned him Kamenwati's respect.

Kamenwati felt the waves of love coming off this small group, and he suddenly liked them all. These were the people that helped to shape his Alicia after the death of her parents, and for that he would always be grateful. He could also feel their curiosity toward him and Conall, but they said nothing.

Alicia's small hand on his forearm was gentle and cool, maybe a little too cool. She would need feeding soon.

Conall glided silently to his side, and then stood as still as a statue, taking in everything around him without giving away a thing. He had a predatory aura that had Kamenwati worried. Did Conall need to feed? How long could a magi stay on earth without the need for blood? The Fates had cursed them all, and Conall was exception to the burning hunger while here on earth.

Kamenwati let his eyes follow the path Conall's took, and spotted the young female he had somehow overlooked earlier. The two older wolves, the taller had a proprietary arm slung casually over the elder *Moarte*'s shoulder, and another young one identical to the male standing with Alicia, who incidentally was still admiring his morning star and did not seem aware of the tension around them, had created a wall with their bodies as they instinctively tried to shield her from Conall's view. Smart move if they could see Conall's aura.

A blast of heat mingled with hunger hung in the air around Conall, and the males growled with low menace.

Conall. The word clipped. Kamenwati felt the hunger and frustration roll off Conall, but the mage did not change position or expression.

In a fluid motion, the *Moarte* shrugged off the large male's arm and stepped forward. The male was tall and muscular, without an ounce of fat anywhere. Although he was older, it was easy to see the resemblance between him and the two youngest males. This was the male who helped raise Alicia and Kamenwati owed him a debt of gratitude. Without the *Moarte* and this male, he would never have met the keeper of his heart.

That the male was torn between protecting his mate and his child would be evident to a blind man. When he took a step toward the *Moarte* she waved him back with a slight movement of her hand, and the next moment she was standing in front of Conall.

" Back off mage," she hissed. " She is not for you."

Conall raised an eyebrow, but was smart enough not to piss off the *Moarte*, again.

"Mom," Alicia and the young female cried simultaneously. The young female pushed her way through the blockade of male bodies; her face pink with embarrassment, and an angry fire glittering in her amber eyes.

Moarte. So that is why he had not detected her immediately. The *Moarte* alone had the ability to travel the universe undetected if they desired to do so. Either way, a *Moarte* this young would be easy to overlook in the presence of an elder *Moarte*.

The female wore form fitting blue jeans and a black top with no sleeves that complemented her pale skin. Her hair hung in a long braid, and although she held no visible weapons Kamenwati knew she was ready to do battle by the way she moved. The way she glared at the towering males around her it was easy to see she was no pushover. She was young, but Kamenwati could feel her power. He hoped she knew how to use that power; it could be a matter of life or death.

Alicia rushed forward and grabbed the girl's hand, urging her forward. She glared at the males, the youngest of which managed to look at least a little contrite. It was easy to imagine these two women growing up together, siding with each other against the males. The rush of love that came over Kamenwati had his golden orbs glowing, and heat was emanating from him making his own golden aura more pronounced.

Alicia's dark eyes met his, and the tip of her tongue traced the curve of her upper lip as it moved over her aching fangs. Hunger glittered in her dark eyes, and Kamenwati's groin tightened. When she spoke her voice came out light, and breathless.

"This is my sister, Emerald," she swallowed. " Em, this is Kamenwati. I hope you will be great friends."

Kamenwati smiled revealing even white teeth against his deep tan, and nodded slightly. "Little sister," he acknowledged, hiding a grin at the way she bristled at the word little. He would have given her a proper welcoming hug but he was aware of the suspicious looks he was receiving from the males. If this were not Alicia's family he would whisk her away from here, and be damn the consequences. But they were her family, and he knew how much they meant to her so he would play nice.

Emerald stared up at the tall Egyptian with the golden orbs. My god he was gorgeous, and the power. This is what she felt coming from the farmhouse. What was he? Definitely not human. Thank god he was on Alicia's side. Emerald did not want to go against such power, not even with her mother at her side. She knew her mother was powerful, but she had no illusions that she was invincible. They were *Moarte*. They were not gods.

Alicia turned to the dark haired man beside Kamenwati, and hesitated. It was only a slight hesitation but Emerald noticed, and by the way the males eyes darkened dangerously, she knew he noticed as well. Alicia narrowed her eyes slightly, and the male's own eyes narrowed menacingly. Kamenwati stiffened at Alicia's side, and the other man shrugged, and raised a brow questioningly.

"This is Conall," Alicia finally said. " Conall's a friend of," another slight hesitation and she said " Kamenwati's."

What aren't you saying, wondered Emerald, and then forgot all about it when she saw the way Conall was looking at her. Like he was hungry, and she was the main course. *No, wait,* that's how she was looking at him. He was absolutely yummy. Not a boy to be flirted with just to rile her brothers, no, he was definitely a male worth knowing.

Conall managed to smile without revealing the fangs that were trying to punch their way out of his mouth. He had forgotten how easily the blood lust could be aroused while on earth, and her blood sang to him like a love song. He stepped forward on stiff legs, and took her hand in his, and lifted it to his lips. He inhaled, savoring the bouquet of her power-enhanced blood racing through her veins before turning her hand over and placing a kiss in her palm.

Emerald was totally mesmerized by the dark sensual look in Conall's eyes as he slowly lifted her hand to his mouth, and then turned it over to place a kiss in her palm. His lips lingered far longer than was necessary, and the heat from his lips scorched her. Her heart skipped a beat, and then started to pound erratically. She wanted to ignore the warning growls behind her, but couldn't quite block them out. *Not now,* she moaned. She nearly cried in disappointment when he finally released her hand, and took a step back.

"Emerald," he said.

It was only her name but he made it sound erotic with his lilting accent. Emerald had to force her attention back to Alicia and the others.

"The one lusting after your morning star," Alicia was saying in a soft teasing voice, "is Gheorgès. He is the eldest of the triplets, and thinks he is in charge."

Gheorgès growled low at Alicia. "Give me a break. I've only ever seen one of these in a museum." He stepped forward to clasp both Kamenwati's forearms, and bent slightly at the waist. "Kamenwati," he acknowledged before turning to Conall and greeting him in the same way.

Conall couldn't help but notice the way the young lycan managed to place his body between Conall and Emerald, as if he just noticed how close they were standing. *Probably a good idea,* he thought. *She is much too tempting, and much too young.* He had not needed the *Moarte's* warning to tell him that.

"The quiet one is my brother Quinn. Don't let his demeanor fool you. He is every bit a warrior as Gheorgès." When Quinn nodded his acknowledgement, she continued. "My father, Luke Wulfson." Her voice echoed her pride and love.

Luke stepped forward and gave his daughter a quick hug and a kiss on the cheek. "Don't think I'm letting you off the hook for worrying your mother, young lady," he scolded her gently, and winked before acknowledging the introductions as Gheorgès had, in the manner of warriors.

Alicia paused before Matthew, a slight furrow to her brow. " Matthew," she finally said. "Matthew works with my mother. He runs the Mexican branch of O'Connor Search and Rescue. He is the one who brought my mother's body home so we could bury it."

Matthew was startled until he realized that Jade would have told her daughter who he was. " Kamenwati, Conall," he acknowledged but did not move forward. "Nice to see you again, Alicia. You have grown into a fine woman. Your parents would have been proud."

Alicia winced slightly as the memories of her parents deaths flashed through her mind. " Thank you Matthew."

The black clouds were gathering over the farmhouse and the air felt cooler, and more stifling at the same time. Emerald looked into the sky, and shuddered.

" Don't worry." She jumped at the sound of Conall's voice at her ear. "He can't reach us until the sun goes down. He needs the full moon to cross over."

How did he get so close without anyone noticing? Gheorgès glared, and Conall shrugged. He was going to move away. Emerald knew it, as well as she knew she did not want him to, and it had nothing to do with the way he made Gheorgès hackles rise. Unlike the boys back home, she found Conall fascinating. Was it because he was more male than anyone she ever met or the power that rolled off him in waves, or the way her blood raced and her heart started doing the tango when he was near? She didn't know what it was the male made her feel, but she wanted to explore the feeling.

" Wait," she whispered when he started to walk off.

Conall stopped and turned back, his dark eyes glittering. He wasn't smiling; rather he looked like he was in pain.

Suddenly unsure of herself, Emerald wished she had just let him walk away.

When she didn't say anything, he lifted his eyes to watch the dark clouds gathering into the large, menacing form of the betrayer. Conall wanted her to say something, anything. Her voice sang to him like a choir of angels, and he could listen to it forever. This was too dangerous. She was too young to realize what she felt, and he was too dangerous in this state.

"The betrayer cannot take corporeal form until the sun goes down." And when it did she would be in danger. They would all be in danger. The urge to protect her hit him like a bolt of lightning. "You should not be here," he snarled startling Emerald with the anger in his voice. "Your parents were unwise to allow you near this danger."

White-hot anger rushed through Emerald's veins, and her vision blurred red. She was not a helpless infant, and she would show him dangerous. She raised her hand, a ball of molten energy forming in her palm. Conall grabbed her wrist. His black orbs locked with her amber ones. Gheorgès leapt.

Conall waved his free hand, and Gheorgès landed on his ass. Emerald wanted to laugh at the stunned look on Gheorgès face but she was angry. Too angry. The anger clawed at her insides until she thought she would throw up. Her head was pounding like a battle drum.

Fight it. She knew she had to fight the anger. It wasn't real. It wasn't hers. But the desire to blast that stunned look off Conall's face was almost uncontrollable. *Oh god, what is happening to me?*

Do it. Blast him. The disembodied voice was unnaturally seductive. The words beat into Emerald's mind until she wanted to obey them. She forced herself to look into Conall's dark glittering eyes filled with worry and strength, and tried to tell him not to worry. At the same time, she felt the need to blast him with enough power to knock him into the shadows.

The shadows.

Quick as a flash, Emerald ripped her wrist from Conall's iron grip, spun around, and sent a blast of energy into the dark form hovering over them. There was a howl of pain and rage, and the cloud ripped apart. Even as she watched the clouds disassemble, they began moving together again.

How dare you try to use my own emotions against me? Emerald's fury turned from Conall, to the shadow, to herself in a heartbeat. Maybe Conall was right and she was only a hindrance to her family.

"You were very brave." Conall's soft lilt did nothing to soothe her temper.

Emerald wouldn't look at Conall. She did not want to see the pity in his ebony eyes. *Weak. That's what I am. Weak and useless. A hindrance to my family and a failure as 'Moarte.' I should have let Daniel take me home.*

"I'm sorry," she said in a shaky voice. "Thank you for stopping me." She didn't wait to hear what he had to say. Emerald stalked over to her mother, her amber eyes troubled. "I'm sorry Mother. I couldn't fight it."

Jade shook her head slightly, and grimaced. She wanted to wrap her arms around her daughter and tell her how strong she was, but that would only embarrass Emerald further, and she would not do that.

"You did fight," she told her in a matter of fact, no nonsense voice. "You did not allow him to control your power."

"I could have hurt him. I could have hurt all of you."

"But you didn't. That is the part you must remember. You did not let Theron control your power through your emotions." Jade took both her daughter's hands in hers, and forced her to look her in the eye. " Remember what it felt like so the next time you can fight it sooner."

"You don't understand Mom. I wanted to kill him. I wanted to hit him with a blast strong enough to send him into the shadows."

Jade tugged at her daughter's hands to make sure she was paying attention. "That was Theron not you. You were angry because you think Conall sees you as a helpless child, and Theron used that anger to his own advantage."

Jade smirked at Emerald's startled look, and gave her head a slight shake. " Do you think for one moment that I do not see the way that male looks at you? Your brothers and father are not the only ones with eyes. Stay away from him Emerald. He is not for you. You are young, with volatile emotions, and our enemies will try to use those emotions against you. You must learn to trust yourself and your feelings, so that this does not happen again."

Emerald glanced at Conall who was deep in conversation with Kamenwati. Suddenly his dusky gaze met hers and she quickly looked away. "It's because he is mage isn't it?"

"That's not the only reason," was all Jade would say on the subject.

Emerald's amber gaze shifted to the dark gathering clouds and her blood ran cold. If Theron held that much control over her what chance would a newly born magi have? She reached out to Alicia.

Be strong.

Thirty

The ground beneath rumbled and rolled as if a massive earthquake shook the very foundation of the world. Chickens squawked and fluttered into the air. Grackles and small Mexican songbirds took to the skies, only to land outside the perimeter of the farm when the dark clouds gathered ominously close. Insects stilled. Fruit trees in the orchard began to wilt; their leaves falling lifelessly to the ground.

The sun was on the downslide. Dusk was coming.

He was coming.

Hurry my children.

The call travelled on silent wings across the universe to every being with a trace of vampire or mage blood. Conall heard the call as clearly as he heard the seductive tones of the betrayer when he attempted to manipulate the *Moarte*.

The betrayer was calling the vampire to him, banding them together. He could feel their movement beneath his feet as they travelled through the bowels of the earth to avoid the killing rays of the sun.

Thirty-One

*B*e strong.

Alicia shivered. Hunger clawed at her insides, and her head ached from all the noise. She was not strong. Conall was strong. She looked at him differently. He was no longer the monster her father sent for her whose only redeeming feature was his friendship with Kamenwati. Now he was a man fighting an evil that was as much a part of her as it was of him, and he had saved her sister while doing it. For that, Alicia owed him a huge debt.

When the seeker had reached out to manipulate Emerald, Alicia was too busy fighting her own desire to sink her fangs into Kamenwati's vein that she could not offer her aid.

Be strong. If only she could. Right now, she felt as weak as a milk-starved kitten. She needed to feed.

Prey. The word rang in her mind and her fangs elongated until she had trouble hiding them behind her lips. The scent of blood was so strong it blocked out everything else. Gone was the sweet fragrance of the morning glory, the tangy scent of pine. The beating of hearts grew so loud she thought she would go insane. If she did not get away, she was going to turn into a monster and attack her own family.

She felt Kamenwati's hand at her back, and the sensations that gentle touch invoked made her knees weak.

You need to feed little one. Hot need rushed through her at the guttural tones.

In a less than subtle move, Kamenwati scooped Alicia into his strong tanned arms and strode purposely toward the farmhouse. "We must prepare." His guttural tones allowed no room for argument.

Alicia hid her face against his broad chest so nobody could see the grin on her face. Never before had anyone dared command her father, and the stunned look on his face made her want to laugh aloud. To his credit, Luke simply nodded, and did not try to stop the Egyptian. Alicia felt giddy and blamed it on hunger for the tall, lean male who held her so close to his heart she could feel its steady beat, and smell the rich powerful blood that beckoned her.

Alicia's fangs punched out past her top lip and scraped gently across the bare skin where his vest had opened slightly. Kamenwati's step faltered. Alicia peeked at him from beneath her long silky lashes, her dark eyes glittering with promise, and something dark and compelling.

Stop that, Kamenwati chided softly in her mind. *Unless you want me to take you right now in front of your family.*

Alicia sighed, and snuggled closer. "You smell good," she said her voice husky. Pushing his vest open further, she nipped at the skin against his beating heart. *Good enough to eat.*

It took every ounce of will power Kamenwati possessed to remember to close the door behind them and throw up the protective chimera around the room before falling to the bed with Alicia sprawled on top of him. When she began to crawl slowly up his long body, slinking like a predator stalking its prey, rubbing her body against his and purring like a kitten, he nearly lost control.

Her tongue flicked in and out. He tasted like dark rich caramel, and her nostrils flared at the dark erotic spice of his arousal. Alicia's answering lust was so powerful she started to shake. The erratic beating of his heart was a beacon calling to her. The rich scent of blood and lust filled the air. Alicia's fangs punched out.

Kamenwati kept himself as still as possible while Alicia crawled along his long frame. The gentle friction had his blood boiling and his arousal in a painful state. He wanted to claim her as his own. He needed to mark her so no other male would dare answer her siren's call.

He flipped Alicia on her back and nuzzled her neck while he rubbed his encouraged sex against her. He started a crawl of his own kissing and licking her exposed flesh as he removed her clothing.

Kamenwati could spend days just suckling those taut nipples, enjoying the way she squirmed and moaned beneath him, but they were running out of time. She needed to feed before nightfall. She was already weakening and unless she was at full strength, she would not be able to resist the betrayer's influence.

I will.

"What?" Kamenwati lifted his head to gaze into her dark hunger filled eyes.

Alicia took a couple of deep breaths letting them out slowly in an attempt to still the rapid beating of her heart. "Resist," she finally said. "I know what he wants me to do and I will never turn on my family or you."

She grimaced and struggled to a sitting position. Her shirt hung open and the pink tip of her rigid nipple was playing peek-a-boob with Kamenwati. "You don't have to worry about Conall either. He saved my sister and for that I will honor him."

Kamenwati wanted to take that taut teasing nipple back into his own hungry mouth and push Alicia down beneath him, instead he moved to sit beside her, and leaned against the beautiful hand carved headboard. Like everything else in the farmhouse, you could see the love in every stroke of the carving knife.

Alicia's hair was a mass of curls and tangles, and Kamenwati could not resist reaching out and running his fingers through it. The instant his fingers touched her hair the tangles unfurled leaving behind smooth bouncing curls.

Alicia snuggled against his shoulder. "Where were you when I was growing up," she murmured.

"Watching from Chimera."

Alicia playfully thumped his shoulder. "Why didn't you do something? There were times I thought my mother was going to make me bald when she tried to get the tangles out."

"I like your hair. It's wild and free."

Her fingers worried at the bed cover beneath her, and she tried to think of anything except the spicy aroma of Kamenwati's rich powerful blood.

"You need to feed," he said and turned his head to offer his throat.

Tears pooled in Alicia's eyes when she looked at him. "Is it always going to be like this? How does Conall do it?"

"Yes." When Alicia cocked one eyebrow, he continued. "It's the change. Your body needs fuel to function properly. In the beginning it is always harder to resist. You will always crave the blood, but you will learn to control your desires. You need to feed or you will become weak and die, or the betrayer will gain control of you and you will be lost forever. He does not care how he gains control of your power as long as he gains it."

"How does he win if I die?" Alicia thought about ending it all so she could never betray her family with her hunger, but she could never do that if it meant helping Kamenwati's enemy.

" When you die your power is released into the universe. The betrayer ..."

"Theron."

Kamenwati's golden orbs widened in surprise. Nobody spoke the betrayer's birth name since the day his father sent him into the Shadows.

"That's his name isn't it? Theron? My uncle?" Her fingers worrying the bed cover suddenly stilled. "That's how he finds me isn't it? We share a blood bond?"

Kamenwati nodded, and Alicia continued. "He sent the vampire that destroyed my mama and papa before my power was even developed because he wanted it for himself." Her hand shot out and a small clay pot sitting on the dresser suddenly flew across the room. It slammed against the far wall disintegrating into a pile of dust. Alicia's fingers wiggled and the pile of powder began to swirl and twirl, taking on the shape of a funnel and starting to dance faster and faster until they became a small cyclone. With a snap of her fingers, the cyclone stilled, and the pile of debris settled.

"Parlor tricks," she said bitterly. " He killed my parents because I can do parlor tricks."

"You are capable of much more than that." Kamenwati barely lifted his index finger to make a circular motion in the direction of the debris. The particles of reddish brown dust gathered until they took on the shape of the small pot, and then they flew across the room to settle on the dresser.

Excitement sparkled in Alicia's dark orbs. " How did you do that?"

"Manipulate the elements. The pot was clay. Made of earth." *You are so beautiful when your eyes glitter like that.*

Alicia snuggled closer, and Kamenwati inhaled her unique fragrance. *You need to feed,* he encouraged silently.

I don't want to. Alicia sounded like a pouty child, but she mentally put her hand up to stall his reply, and added. *I said I didn't want to not that I wouldn't.* She shifted around until her fangs gently scraped the flesh covering his heart, and she hesitated. Peace enveloped her at the gentle voice in her head that drowned out the malicious urgings of Theron.

I offer what is mine to give. My heart, my soul, my life.

I take into my keeping that which is offered. Your heart, your soul, your life, answered Alicia. *I offer my heart, my soul, and my life into your keeping.*

From this moment forward, you shall be the keeper of my heart, my soul, and my life, they said in unison.

There was a blast of brilliant light, and Alicia felt something inside her shift. It felt almost as if something warm and comforting had settled in her chest.

" Drink," Kamenwati urged.

This time Alicia let her fangs pierce the skin protecting his heart. The first pull was a hit of ecstasy. Power surged through her veins making her stronger, more powerful— alive. How had she not wanted this? With every sip came power and knowledge, ancient knowledge she could only dream about. She saw what was in Kamenwati's mind, and felt what was in his heart.

Alicia had finally come home.

"No!" Theron's molecules scattered across the heavens in fury and frustration. Thunder rumbled. Lightning flashed.

How dare he? She was his. His blood. The key to his return. For centuries he had been stuck in the shadows, a part of everything, and yet nothing at all. Each day he plotted and planned his revenge on Ra, and his pansy assed sibling Alaric. Prince of the Magi, ha, he was nothing but a chess piece in this game between Ra and himself.

He spent eons gathering the power he needed to break free of this prison. He crawled like a worm through innocent minds, warping and corroding until they became mindless vessels whose only desire was to do his bidding. Those he couldn't corrupt he had destroyed, thus releasing their power back into the universe where he could absorb it.

He would have her power. He would not let the bastard offspring of that pious Ra cheat him of that. This was going to be fun. By destroying her, he would destroy the heart of his brother, and bring down Ra through his son.

Come my children, he commanded. *Destroy her. Destroy them all, and together we will rule the world.*

Thirty-Two

Emerald entered the gloom of the old musty barn, and listened to the whisper of wings as the starlings in the rafters shifted position. There was a rustle of hay and a small brown mouse scampered out of the safety of the prickly hay, and stopped to stare up at Emerald with its beady little eyes. Emerald stared back, her eyes narrowing into slits. The mouse suddenly squeaked, and scampered back into the safety of the deep hay.

Emerald laughed.

" So the mean pussy cat scares the poor little mouse."

Emerald spun around at the soft lilting voice, her face mottled with embarrassment. Conall was standing nearly hidden by a pile of hay in a darkened corner of the barn sharpening the edge of a lethal looking blade. "How? What?" She stammered, took a deep breath, and said. " What are you talking about," in the haughtiest voice she could muster.

Conall ran his thumb along the well-honed edge, and nodded with satisfaction. He tucked the blade into the sheath on the side of one tall black boot, and pulled out a second blade from the other boot. After eyeing it from different angles, he meticulously began sharpening it.

"You made that poor little mouse think you were a large tabby, a very hungry large tabby, and nearly gave it a heart attack." There was no condemnation in his voice. He was simply stating a fact as if he didn't care one way or the other about her or the mouse.

Emerald walked to the back of the barn slowly, letting her eyes adjust to the gloom. " Does the light hurt your eyes?" she asked. "I mean…"

Conall shrugged. "Sometimes. I am not vampire, Emerald. I do not sizzle in the sun, or drain my prey. I am Magi and therefore not subject to the same laws of nature."

Emerald felt her cheeks burning, and shifted uncomfortably. Why did she have to say something so stupid? She knew he was not vampire. "I'm sorry," she began when Conall stalled her.

"I am Magi." He lifted is head to see her more clearly, his glittering ebony eyes almost caressing her pale face. "I'm not vampire, Emerald, but that does not mean I am not dangerous." He thrust the newly honed blade into the pocket of his boot, and suddenly his fangs punched past his lips distorting is handsome features, and revealing his hunger.

Conall moved like lighting. One moment he was standing in the shadows a few feet away, the next he was leaning close enough to kiss her—or bite her. " Go back to your family, Emerald," he hissed. " Before it is too late and I change my mind."

He turned on his heel and strode deeper into the shadows.

Thirty-Three

The sun dropped behind the horizon like a stone. The ground beneath their feet trembled slightly. Jade shoved Luke away from her and leapt to the sky, shifted and returned to earth with her claws extended.

The earth where they were standing just a moment before exploded spewing dirt and rocks like shrapnel. A pale figure burst from the hole, its dark eyes glittered with hunger as it dove toward Luke. Luke shifted to wolf and leapt to meet the attack even as the white owl's talons dug into the back of the vampire's neck. The vampire screamed and twisted sideways missing the owl as it fell to the ground, and barely avoiding the large sharp teeth of the two hundred pound grey wolf.

Behind them, the farmhouse door blew open with a blast and Kamenwati hurled a fireball at a second vampire as it tried to escape the earth. Thunder rumbled, and the earth shook as a large black coach came barreling from the skies pulled by two enormous black bears. Behind Kamenwati Alicia froze in terror as the creatures from her nightmares dove straight for her. In less than a heartbeat, she shook off the terror to shove Kamenwati out of the way of those massive claws and teeth. She leaped in the opposite direction, turning to throw a blast of energy at the bears even as they tried to avoid hitting the farmhouse. The coach behind them was not so lucky. It caught the edge of the wall, and slats of ebony showered down like arrows piercing the earth. Theron's image hovered above the debris, and slowly took corporeal form.

Alicia stared at her uncle's nearly transparent form in awe and hatred. The power glowed around him like a full body halo. He could easily be the most handsome man she had ever seen if it was not for the sneer on his face, and the pure evil that emanated from him like a living breathing entity. Alicia stared, transfixed by that evil, listening to its seductive voice in her head while Theron tried to manipulate her.

My child, his insipid voice whispered. *Join us. We are your true family. These people are not your family. They lie to you. They only want to exploit your meager power. I do not. I am your family. We are your family. We have no need of your power. We are already powerful. Come to me my child and I will protect you from harm.*

The voice in her head mesmerized Alicia. The seductive, hypnotic tones travelled through her, urging her forward, and her legs acted as if they were no longer her own. First one step, and then another as her traitorous legs carried her closer to the monster that beckoned her. She was not aware of anyone or anything except the voice in her head.

What was only a moment in time felt like an eternity as Alicia slowly moved toward Theron on legs that refused to obey her. With each step closer she took, the figure grew more substantial until she could no longer see Kamenwati and the others through his form.

Several vampires surrounded Kamenwati who swung his morning star with ease, smashing them bloodied and useless to the ground. His foot shot out behind him and he rolled, jamming his heel with its spiked edge into another vampire's throat. The vampire fell to the ground, clasping its emaciated hands against the jagged edges of its torn throat, and tried to hold its life force in even as it sputtered and gurgled, and seeped into the earth.

A ball of energy hit the ground as Kamenwati rolled out of the way and flipped to his feet. His returning blast missed its target and landed mere inches from Theron's feet.

Stop! Alicia ordered her wayward limbs, pleading silently with herself the way she pleaded with her poor papa so many years ago. *See him for what he is. Do not go to him.*

An energy ball twirled above Kamenwati's palm, increasing in size while he searched for an opportunity to dispatch it toward Theron without risking the chance of hitting Alicia. Two vampires chose that moment to attack from opposite directions. Kamenwati released the energy ball at one. The smell of burning flesh filled the air even as Kamenwati spun around slashing his morning star through the air and knocking the other vampire six feet back. It lay on the ground one arm was twisted awkwardly at its side. The other arm rose slowly, its fingers dancing in the air as it tried to call forth the energies of the universe.

A lethal blade flew straight as an arrow into the black heart of the vile creature. Conall stepped forward and his sword flashed, easily separating the creature's head from its body. He spun on his heel and began slashing his way to where Emerald and her brothers were fighting.

An energy blast struck Quinn in the forearm. Pain screamed through his arm and his knife fell uselessly to the ground. In a flash of power, he shifted and leapt. All teeth and claws he landed on the nearest vampire and ripped out its throat. Gheorgès appeared instantly with his sword in his hand and Quinn backed off to allow his brother to finish the decapitation with a graceful swipe of his sword.

Gheorgès turned to see Matthew surrounded by vampires. He only took two steps before a large white owl and an even larger grey wolf entered the fray. There was an angry roar overhead. Two gigantic black bears were bearing down on them. Saliva dripped from their long white fangs, and steam blew from their nostrils. They aimed straight for Emerald and Quinn who had their backs turned and were busy with a half dozen vampires.

Alicia was so close to Theron she could smell his putrid odor. He smelled like death and destruction. He smiled in triumph and his glistening fangs dripped yellow. *That's right my child. Come to me.*

Alicia's blood ran icy hot as memories flashed through her mind. Her childhood spent in fear. Papa and Mama destroyed by vampires at her uncle's command. The nearer she got to Theron the angrier she grew, until she was no longer fighting the movement of her legs. Instead, she went with them, letting their momentum carry her to her target.

She was so close now Theron could reach out and take her. He looked into her white-hot eyes and his blood froze, and his step faltered. He wanted to turn and run. He wanted to open a portal and return to the safety of the Shadows. He took a faltering step toward her.

"That's it you bastard," she taunted in a voice that was deadly quiet. "You wanted me. Come and get me." Pure energy streamed from her eyes, her mouth, even her hair stood on end as the energy poured through the strands before escaping into the atmosphere. Alicia focused that white-hot gaze on her uncle—and smiled.

Theron screamed.

A ribbon of pure white energy hung in the air between them, binding them together. Theron struggled to free himself from its hold. The blood in his veins began to boil. He had underestimated her power, her control, and it could cost him his life. It was not fair. Once again, his pansy-assed brother was going to win without ever having to lift a finger.

There was a small popping sound, less the noise of a kernel of popping corn busting out of its shell, and just before Theron's corporeal form exploded into millions of molecules blowing in the wind, he heard. *Goodbye, brother.*

"No!" His scream echoed through the universe even as he was cast back into the Shadows.

Alicia's legs felt like jelly, and she collapsed into the comforting arms of oblivion.

In the Chimera, Alaric staggered and dropped to his ass with a thump. Ra settled far more gracefully on the stone floor at his side. The Eye of Ra shimmered and rippled, distorting his view of earth before blinking closed the connection.

"You did well my friend." Ra snuck a sideways glance to assure him that his longtime friend would suffer no long-term effects of expending so much power. He did not like the gray pallor of his skin, or the exhaustion he saw in his eyes.

"He should never have gone after my daughter." Alaric let his exhaustion take over, and closed his eyes. He was unconscious before his head hit the floor.

Ra lifted his friend gently as if he were a newborn babe, and carried him home.

Thirty-Four

The gigantic paws pounded the earth like thunder across the hard surface. It sounded like a train wreck waiting to happen as the beast bore down on Emerald and Quinn. Emerald heard the thunderous footsteps coming straight for them. She felt the beast's hot putrid breath on the nape of her neck and turned to face the ursaline monster, trusting Quinn to keep the vampires from her back.

Everything happened in slow motion. Gheorgès was too far away to help. Even as he shifted and leaped to intercept the beast she knew he was not going to make it. Jade and Luke were across the yard fighting a half dozen or so vampire who had failed to beat a hasty retreat at their master's defeat. Kamenwati was lifting Alicia's limp form from the ground.

Oh god. What happened to Alicia? Emerald was so intent on her battle with the vampire that she did not have a clue what was happening around her. She reached out to her sister, and let out a sigh of relief when she detected a strong heartbeat. *Exhaustion.* Alicia would live.

Emerald stared into the fanatical eyes of the beast and was not so sure about her own future. The beast intended to tear her apart limb by limb, and devour the remains. The image in her mind was so strong she could feel the bear's claws raking her body, and its teeth tearing into her unprotected flesh.

With a shudder, she shook off the image, and shot a blast of energy at the bear. It shook the blast off as if it was no more than a housefly buzzing around, and snarled. Saliva dripped from its jowls.

The bear's black eyes locked with hers and she saw herself helplessly shifted into owl form only to be swatted to the ground, and her white feathers fluttered in the wind as her crimson blood seeped into the ground.

To her horror, the bear actually seemed to smirk at her, and the scenario changed. Emerald shifted to her wolf form, and instantly the bear's massive paw shot out and raked its claws down her side. The wound was fatal, and she screamed as crimson rivers ran through her white fur. She lay on her side, panting as death slowly and painfully claimed her.

"No." Emerald shouted in order to shake off the hallucinations. What sort of creature was this that could shift into the form of the bear, and possessed such powers?

The bear blinked, pawed the ground, and leaped for her throat. Before Emerald could react to the sudden change in tactics, she felt herself shoved to the side. She hit the ground rolling, and screamed as the bear's massive jaws closed over Conall's head. The sound of crushing bone drowned out all other sounds of battle.

A huge black wolf pounced through the air and locked its jaws in the back of the bear's neck. The bear roared in fury and released its hold on Conall's head. The bear tossed its head back and forth in a futile attempt to dislodge the wolf's hold. Emerald called to the energy surrounding her intending to blast the creature with enough power to incinerate it, when her mother's calm voice whispered in her head. *No magic. He can absorb and use whatever you throw at him.*

Emerald released the energy back into the atmosphere and grabbed Conall's sword where it lay on the ground beside his limp form. With a strength born of fury and despair, she thrust the sword up to the hilt into the side of the massive black beast. Hot blood spurted covering her arms and her face; it ran like a river as it turned the ground crimson. The beast thrashed and howled. Gheorgès clamped tighter on its neck, grinding his jaws as he tried to chew through the large spinal cord. The bear rose on its hind legs in another attempt to dislodge Gheorgès. Quinn's wolf took advantage of the unprotected underside, and attacked. Emerald slashed at the beast with Conall's sword. After what seemed an eternity the beast fell to the ground, shuddered once, and stilled.

Emerald rushed to where Conall lay in a pool of his own blood. She called forth the energy around her and fused the shattered pieces of his skull, squelching the blood flow. His heartbeat was almost imperceptible.

"Don't die," Emerald sobbed. She held Conall's head on her lap, her tears dripping onto his pale, still face. Anger surged through her. This was all her fault. Once again, she let her enemy mesmerize her, and this time Conall was paying with his life. "Don't you dare die, Conall," she ordered her voice desperate with fear. "I am not going to let you die."

The index finger on her left hand grew into a lethal looking talon, and she sliced her right wrist with it. She shoved the gaping wound into Conall's mouth. " Drink damn you," she ordered.

Relief flooded her when he convulsively swallowed the warm liquid as it trickled down the back of his throat. His lips clamped over the open wound and he began to suck savagely. Emerald began to feel faint, and then grew frightened when he would not release her wrist, but she would not hurt him to save herself. She had hurt him too much already.

There was a flash of light in the sky, and the clouds parted. " Come home my son," a disembodied voice said.

Conall released his hold on Emerald's wrist. His body shimmered for a moment, and then he disappeared.

Thirty-Five

"I can't believe you let that bloodsucker drink from you." Gheorgès wrapped gauze around the jagged tear on Emerald's wrist, and pulled tight enough to make his sister wince.

"That bloodsucker as you call him saved my life."

"I'm sorry, Em," he said his voice contrite.

Emerald wondered if he was sorry for her wound, or for calling Conall a bloodsucker when he immediately loosened the gauze. She winced again when she saw how rapidly the white material turned crimson. She wished she could heal her own wounds as easily as she did those of others. The look on Gheorgès face had her worried. *Why wouldn't the bleeding stop?* Emerald felt dizzy and weak, and was having a hard time keeping her eyes open and her body in a sitting position.

The last few of vampires escaped into the underground tunnels, sealing the entrance behind them. "Let them go," Jade said when Luke and Matthew began digging.

The large gray wolf began to shimmer, and Luke stood staring at the spot in the earth where the vampires vanished. Over by the orchard a small grackle whistled. Luke swatted an annoying mosquito. "Damn bloodsuckers," he muttered.

The smaller black timber wolf inclined its head slightly in agreement. Neither was sure if they meant the mosquito or the vampires. Their heads turned toward the sound of Gheorgès' voice.

"That fucking bloodsucker is lucky it's gone or I'd rip its throat out." Gheorgès glanced at his sister's extremely pale face, and dull amber eyes, and cursed again. Her utter lack of response to his cursing worried him more than he let on. She looked like she was going to fall over at any moment, and her heartbeat was slowing, and becoming more erratic. Already she had lost too much blood, and he could not get the wound to stop bleeding no matter how tight he held the gauze.

"Let me." Jade put a gentle hand on her eldest son's shoulder. When Gheorgès reluctantly released his hold on Emerald's wrist blood spurted from the wound once again soaking the gauze. Jade carefully unwound the gauze and placed her palm over the wound. Shimmering white light glowed between her palm and her daughter's wrist, and the edges of her skin knit together stanching the blood loss.

Sleep my baby, she sent the compulsion.

Emerald's long lashes fluttered, and then drifted down to cover her pale amber eyes. Luke scooped his daughter into his arms before she toppled over, and carried her to Matthew's jeep. The black timber wolf trotted behind the house, and Matthew emerged dressed in blue jeans and a black t-shirt. He walked over to the jeep and slid into the driver's side.

Prepare the guest rooms Theresa. Company's coming.
Already done my love came the instant reply.

Kamenwati listened to the jeep as it kicked up stone and dirt in its haste to leave. *Take care of our daughter, Godson.* The *Moarte*'s voice was both demanding and trusting.

Yes. Kamenwati sat on the bed beside Alicia, and she snuggled against him in her sleep. *Tell little sister Conall lives thanks to her.* The young one would want to know. She blamed herself for something she had no control over, and Conall would not want her to suffer so.

I will. Jade sent Kamenwati an image of her narrowing her eyes fiercely. *Kamenwati, bring her home soon. We miss her.* The brilliant amber eyes sparkled with mischief. *Welcome to the family.*

Welcome to the family. Kamenwati was gazing at Alicia when her dark eyes opened, and she smiled at him.

"You really don't know what you are getting into," she sighed. Her voice was raspy and she coughed slightly.

" Do you need to drink?"

"I need something," she teased. Alicia wriggled her way up Kamenwati's long body, stopping to torture him when she reached his engorged sex, and smiled seductively. Her dark eyes sparkled with lust, and something mysterious. "I'd settle for a glass of water." At Kamenwati's disappointed expression, she hastily added, "for now."

Kamenwati wanted her to stay exactly where she was. He held his palm up and a tall glass of clear cool water appeared.

Alicia lowered her lashes, and chewed on her lower lip. "I wanted water from our well," she said petulantly. When the glass was replaced with another, she quickly added. "In my own cup."

She laughed when her old tin cup appeared in Kamenwati's palm.

Kamenwati bowed his head, his golden eyes gleaming. "Your majesty." He did a perfect imitation of a lady-in-waiting at a palace. "I hope you find my humble offering to your liking."

Alicia smiled revealing the tips of her fangs. The tip of her tongue peeked past her blood red lips as it traced the outline of her teeth. She grinned wickedly when Kamenwati shifted to ease the tightness in his balls, and wiggled her eyebrows in a bad imitation of *Snidley Whiplash,* and twirled an imaginary moustache. " What exactly are you offering?"

"Me."

"Mmmm." Alicia leaned in and slowly licked the side of his neck. " A tasty offering." She took the pitted tin cup that was wobbling precariously on his palm, and drank the sweet fresh water. "Thank you kind sir," she said.

With a nonchalant wave of her hand, the cup began to drift across the room. Alicia didn't wait for it to settle beside the clay pot on the dresser. She leaned forward and captured Kamenwati's mouth, letting her tongue explore its warm cavern. He tasted hot and spicy, like his blood.

Ignoring the hunger clawing at her insides she took her time exploring his sensuous mouth before nibbling her way past his jaw to his throat.

Kamenwati tensed when her fangs scraped over the vein in his neck, anticipating the sharp stinging pain of her fangs piercing his skin before it turned into the most erotic feeling he could imagine.

Her teeth scraped the edge of the vein, and then moved down until she was nibbling at his collarbone, and lower. He jumped when she nipped the tip of his tender nipple, his clothes having vanished with a mere touch of her hand. Kamenwati chuckled. "You're getting good at that."

"That's not all I'm good at," she returned. Her head disappeared down his lean frame. Her tongue licked at his iron hard abs before dipping and twirling around his belly button. His cock, free of its confining clothing reached for the heat of her inner core, but Alicia slid down and caught the tip between her teeth.

Kamenwati moaned and jerked as she slowly sucked in the entire length of him. When she began to let him out, he wanted to knot his fingers into her long silky tangles, and hold her where she was. Instead, he dug his long fingers into the mattress at his sides, and let her play. Lightning wracked his body. He loved what she was doing to him with her mouth and wanted it to last forever, but his balls tightened, his body tensed and jerked, and he ejaculated into those warm depths like a teenager experiencing sex for the first time.

Alicia lifted her head her eyes drowsy with lust. "My turn," she whispered huskily. He watched her with lowered lashes as she crawled back up his lean length, and impaled herself on his still swollen cock.

Kamenwati couldn't think of anything more beautiful that Alicia riding him, her head thrown back, her eyes half closed, her lips slightly parted, and her long tresses brushing the sensitive skin of his upper thighs. He was on the verge of another orgasm when her head suddenly lifted and she looked at him with wild eyes, her fangs already elongated. He tilted his head slightly, offering the pulsing vein at his throat. When those sharp fangs pierced the skin and she drew in the first taste of his blood, they both fragmented into a thousand pieces.

Much later, lying exhausted side by side, Kamenwati pulled Alicia closer against his lean frame, and playfully nibbled on her ear. " What is your answer?"

Alicia blinked up at him, her dark eyes slumberous and confused. " Answer?"

" Will you have me?"

"I just did, didn't I?" She sighed, and snuggled closer. He smelled like blood, sex, and something very much like home.

"I hope you want a big wedding," Kamenwati said.

Thirty-Six

Alicia paced the long cavernous chamber in her diaphanous pink gown listening to the sound of her heels clicking the cold stone floor. *What is going on in there?* She sent the question through the air for the hundredth time.

They are still negotiating, came Kamenwati's calm voice.

You mean they are still arguing. Alicia tried to hide it but she was worried about Luke. Alaric was very powerful, and she did not trust him. He might be her biological father but Luke was her dad, and she wanted him to walk her down the aisle, no matter what the stranger who seduced and then deserted her mother said. She did not care if he was the Prince of the Magi. He was nothing to her.

Do not fret, little one. I will allow no harm to come to your father.

Which one? Alicia snapped sarcastically. Kamenwati's warm chuckle was almost as good as a hug right now. She could not believe they insisted she stay in this room all alone while that *man* decided whether her own family could attend her wedding. This was her wedding. Her wishes should be the only ones that counted.

The lycan of course, he assured.

Alaric had better not lay a finger on Luke, she warned sending an image of teeth and claws floating through Kamenwati's mind. *He will deal with me if he does.*

Kamenwati sighed. *That is what he hopes.*

Alicia growled, and Kamenwati's warm voice wrapped around her like a loving caress. *I love you.*

In another chamber in the palace, Alaric faced Luke with eyes that glittered angrily. He wanted to blast the usurper into the Shadows with his brother, but Kamenwati and Ra had both assured him that was not the way to win his daughter's affections. God she was beautiful. The spitting image of his beautiful Maria with her dark round eyes, pale face, and black curly tresses that refused to be tamed—like her spirit. He understood why she wanted nothing to do with him, but still it hurt, and he would not allow her indifference to continue.

"Look. This is getting us absolutely nowhere." Luke's spoke calmly although all he wanted to do was rip this bloodsucker's throat out. "Alicia specifically made me promise I would walk her down the aisle, and I agreed. Bottom line, I will not break a promise to my daughter." When Alaric's eyes began to glow, Luke hastily added, "You would not break a promise and you cannot expect me to."

"She is my daughter," Alaric spit out through teeth clamped hard together in an attempt to stay calm.

"You donated the sperm, that's all. A father is someone who nurtures, and protects. Where were you when her and her mother needed you?" Luke rolled his eyes, and shook his head in frustration. "Forget I said that. What is past is past. Today is her wedding day, and I am going to walk her down the aisle whether I do it here or in our realm, it makes no difference to me. Here you get to be a part of her big day and I do not have to break my promise. In our realm I still do no break my promise, but you do not get to be a part of it."

Alaric opened his mouth to argue but Kamenwati spoke first. "Enough," he commanded wanting the argument to end before it turned into bloodshed. "The ceremony takes place here and her family will be in attendance." *It is settled, little one. The ceremony is in the hour.*

Jade helped Emerald zip up her pale green silk gown. It clung to her small breasts and then fell loosely to wrap around her lithe form. Her white blonde hair was piled high in a mass of curls that were already loosening to fall in silken wisps down her back. " You look absolutely beautiful, Emmy," she said. " So grown up you make me realize I will soon lose you too."

Emerald forced a smile to her pale pink lips that did not quite reach her amber eyes. " Thanks, mom," she said in a dull voice. " But I'm not going anywhere any time soon."

She glanced at her mother and realized for the first time that Jade was still wearing her bright yellow t-shirt, and brown cargo pants, but at least her feet were bare; nobody wore shoes in the ceremonial chamber. Her eyes widened slightly, and she said in an almost scandalized voice. "Mom! You cannot go to the wedding like that."

Jade looked down at her bare feet, wriggled her toes, and frowned. "There, I painted my toenails."

Emerald was still laughing when Mrs Gray entered the room Alaric had reluctantly designated for the females. "What's the joke?"

"Mom's toes," Emerald snickered. " She painted them for the wedding."

Charlotte Gray glanced down at Jade's toes and burst out laughing. She was so glad she had agreed to let Randy and Sue watch The Inner Sanctum for the month so she could be here. Each toenail was painted with a different food. There were pork chops, steaks, chicken, and even some fruits and vegetables. "Looks like someone is hungry," she said with a wink at Emerald.

Charlotte pulled a powder blue gown from its hanger, and shook it out. " Come on, Jade. The sooner we get you into this dress, the sooner we can get this show on the road. First the vows and then you eat." She glanced at the toes and her round face broke into a wide grin. " Do something with those toes."

Jade shrugged and her polish turned a pale blue that matched her gown. "Is that better?" When Emerald and Charlotte nodded in agreement, she continued. "How is Alicia?" she asked. She would have loved to be a fly on the wall during the meeting with the Prince of the Magi, but he had refused permission for anyone to enter their realm, only agreeing to the meeting with Luke when Kamenwati pressured him. Jade and Luke knew how Alicia felt about the mage that sired her, she did not even try to hide her feelings. Alicia wanted to be married at The Inner Sanctum in Willow Bend. She only agreed that the ceremony take place in the Chimera when Kamenwati told her his father could not be a part of the wedding if it took place on earth, but she had insisted her own family be granted permission to enter the Chimera for the occasion.

The wedding was going to be huge. Every mage would attend to witness the bonding between the son of Ra and the daughter of their prince. The only 'outsiders' were Alicia's family, and Charlotte who Alicia had insisted was like her grandmother. Alicia had graciously agreed that Alaric could perform the ceremony, as was the tradition of the Magi, feeling charitable now that he had conceded to her wishes about her family.

Jade was glad Luke and Kamenwati were able to convince Alaric to permit them in the Chimera for the occasion. Whether Alicia liked it or not she was Magi, and Alaric was a part of her life. She would have to learn to deal with him, and Jade did not want her to regret any decisions she might make right now to keep him away.

A gong sounded, and there was a rap at the door. Jade opened the door, her blood heated up, and her bones began to melt. Luke stood in the doorway dressed immaculately in a dark suit; his dark eyes sparkled with desire as he watched the way his mate's pale blue gown caressed her in all the places he would like to be touching. He swallowed, and bowed offering his arm. "May I have the pleasure of escorting you to the chapel?"

Behind him Gheorgès, looking decidedly uncomfortable in his monkey suit, and Quinn who wore his as comfortably as a second skin were waiting to escort Emerald and Charlotte to the wedding.

Magi of every shape and size filled the chapel, but Emerald knew the moment she entered that *he* was not present. He called to her in his pain, screaming in agony and need, and she could not go to him to ease his burden. The Magi refused to let her go to him, or even tell her where he was, not that she could blame them. She was the cause of his pain, and the reason he was even fighting this battle for his life.

Kamenwati stood at the altar, his golden skin glowing, wearing a simple loincloth that only enhanced his male beauty. He wore thick golden bracelets on each arm with hieroglyphics depicting the history of Ra. The sun tattoo on his chest was glowing so brilliantly it was the only illumination needed in the vast chamber, and yet every two feet a black sconce on the wall held either a blood red or white candle that flickered merrily causing their shadows to dance on the walls and floor.

Ra stood beside his son resplendent in his own simple loincloth his own wristbands discarded during this sacred of ceremonies. He let his eyes roam over the sea of black clad males and white clad females in the chapel, and then across at the pastel colored gowns worn by the *Moarte*, her daughter, and their friend. *Moarte*. Angel of Death. Death Dealers. There were many names given their kind, mostly unwarranted. He scrutinized the young female closely, and liked what he saw. She was young, a babe by their standards, and a child still even in human terms. Yet she had faced the Ursaline as valiantly as any seasoned warrior, and then graciously offered her own life's essence to save one of his children. He owed her a great debt for saving.

A hush fell over the room as Alicia entered, resplendent in a blood-red gown that fell to the floor completely hiding her bare feet. Her dark curls tumbled down her back in a cascade of wild tangles. Her dark eyes shone brightly against her pale face, and her lips matched the shade of her gown. The tips of her fangs peeked out when she smiled at the tall dark lycan waiting just inside the entrance. The love and respect she felt for the male was evident in those expressive eyes.

Alaric bristled from his place at the altar. Alicia seemed to sense it, and faced him. Her smile was not quite as bright as the one she held for the lycan, and did not quite reach her eyes, but it was a start. She accepted the arm the lycan offered, and together they made their way down the aisle to where Kamenwati waited, his own eyes reflecting his love for the petite female who held his heart in the palm of her hand.

Thirty-Seven

It was dark and cold as a grave. The smell of earth filled his nostrils, and he could hear the scratching of tiny feet as they tunneled their way through the rock.

They were coming for him.

They were coming for her.

The taste of sour milk filled his mouth as he fought desperately to get back to her. She had tasted so sweet, so powerful. Her blood was ambrosia, a drug with a stranglehold on him. He wanted more ... needed more.

He could not let them get to her. She was his, and he would save her.

The Angel of Death was near. He could feel her presence in every breath he struggled to take; her presence was both calming and terrifying.

He did not want to die—not yet—not until he tasted her sweet ambrosia one more time. He had to save her from them.

You will taste her, my son, the voice in his head promised. The sound of that voice was almost more terrifying than dying before he saw her again. She would be safe if he died.

You will drain her. That strangely familiar voice insisted. *You will drain them all.*

Coming Next

Blood Obsession

He was helpless, strapped to the stainless steel table; held immobile by silver cuffs burning the skin on his wrists and ankles. The scent of chloroform, disinfectant, and blood—his blood—sickened him. A whisper reached his ears when the door slid open. The smell of rot reached his nose. A smell so strong it masked all the others. It was *his* smell. A smell he would not soon forget.

His tormentor crossed the room without as much as a whisper of sound. With quick, efficient movements, he patted the vein in his arm, drawing it to the surface. The chill of his fingers burned almost as much as the shackles and he wore the stench of the vampire. A long silver tube was plunged in his pulsating vein. He could not stop his scream of agony, and hated the malicious, triumphant smile it brought to his tormentor's grey lips.

He was suffering the fires of hell, only he was on earth. Or was he in hell? Had he crossed over into the afterlife? Had his tormentor finally drained him of his life force?

He forced himself to concentrate on his tormentor—to ignore the pain, and remember.

He was alive. He was Conall. He could feel his blood slowly seeping from his body. His vision blurred. The room darkened.

The Angel of Death was coming for him. The most beautiful angel he had ever seen. Her platinum hair had streaks of gold and silver. Her amber eyes wore the shadows of her pain—his pain. She was flying toward him. He could feel her searching for him. He saw her hair streaming out around her feathers, a mist so delicate as to be nearly undetectable.

He would know his angel anywhere, and in any form. She was so close this time. If only he could hold on until she found him.

He had to hold on until he found her.

LaVergne, TN USA
23 November 2009
165040LV00004B/8/P